HEART OF DARKNESS

&

SELECTIONS FROM THE CONGO DIARY

Joseph Conrad

Heart of Darkness

&

Selections from

The Congo Diary

Introduction by Caryl Phillips

THE MODERN LIBRARY

NEW YORK

1999 Modern Library Paperback Edition

Biographical note copyright © 1993 by Random House, Inc.
Introduction copyright © 1999 by Caryl Phillips

Owing to limitations of space, acknowledgments of permission
to quote from published materials will be found on page 111.

LIBRARY OF CONGRESS CATALOGING-IN-PUBLICATION DATA
Conrad, Joseph, 1857–1924.
[Heart of darkness]
Heart of darkness and selections from The Congo diary/Joseph Conrad;
introduction by Caryl Phillips.—1999 Modern Library pbk. ed.
p. cm.
ISBN 0-375-75377-X (alk. paper)
1. Europeans—Africa—Fiction. 2. Conrad, Joseph, 1857–1924—Journeys—
Zaire. 3. Conrad, Joseph, 1857–1924—Diaries. 4. Zaire—Description and travel.
5. Suffering—Fiction. I. Conrad, Joseph, 1857–1924. Congo diary. II. Title.
PR6005.04H4   1999
823'.912—dc21   99-11703

Modern Library website address: www.modernlibrary.com

Printed in the United States of America

8 9 7

JOSEPH CONRAD

Joseph Conrad was born Józef Teodor Konrad Korzeniowski in Russian-occupied Poland on December 3, 1857. His parents were aristocrats and intensely nationalistic political activists who were exiled to Vologda, northeast of Moscow, for their opposition to tsarist rule. Józef's mother, Ewa, died in 1865 of tuberculosis, and his father, Apollo, succumbed to the same disease four years later. Józef was cared for by his uncle, Tadeusz Bobrowski, until the young man acted on a long-expressed desire to go to sea. In 1874 he left for Marseilles, where he began sailing for the French merchant service.

In 1878, in money difficulties and no longer able to sail on French vessels because he had not secured an exemption from military service in Russia, Conrad attempted suicide. After his recovery, he left Marseilles on a British ship and went to England, where he worked the route between Lowestoft and Newcastle. He arrived in England virtually without qualifications and with very little English, but he was able in a few years to earn his master's certificate in the British merchant marine and became a British national. Conrad traveled to Mauritius and Constantinople, worked on wool clippers from London to Australia, and sailed the waters of the Far East.

These voyages were punctuated by long periods when he could not find suitable positions because of the decline in sail-powered transport in the age of the steamship.

Conrad began writing in English, which became his language of choice after his native Polish and French, although he complained of difficulties with English grammar and syntax. His voyages provided the background for much of his fiction. "Youth" and "Typhoon" draw on Conrad's personal experience with disasters at sea. In 1881, he became second mate on the *Palestine*, a ship that was rammed, caught in tempestuous gales in the English Channel, had its cargo of coal catch fire, and sank off Sumatra. His captaincy of the *Otago* from Bangkok in 1888 informs *The Shadow-Line* (1917) and the stories "Falk" and "The Secret Sharer." "Heart of Darkness" (1899) is drawn from an expedition to the Belgian Congo in 1890. He was already working on a novel when he traveled to the Congo, where he expected to take command of a river steamer. The assignment failed to materialize and Conrad fell dangerously ill. On his return to England, he was forced to find work as a ship's mate. He was able during this period of intermittent employment to devote more time to his writing, and in 1894 he submitted the novel *Almayer's Folly* to the publisher Fisher Unwin. Unwin published it in 1895 under the anglicized version of Conrad's Polish name.

Conrad was encouraged to continue to write by Unwin's reader Edward Garnett, although he went on applying for posts as a ship's captain. He finished *The Outcast of the Islands* in 1895 and in 1896 married Jessie George. They had two sons, Borys and John, born in 1898 and 1906. Constantly in need of more money, Conrad produced short stories and serialized his novels. Although plagued by physical illness and psychological problems, he established one of the most formidable bodies of work in the English language. His longer works include *The Nigger of the "Narcissus"* (1897), *Lord Jim* (1900), *Nostromo* (1904), *The Secret Agent* (1907), *Under Western Eyes* (1911), and *Victory* (1915). From early in his career Conrad had the admiration of fellow writers—Stephen Crane, John Galsworthy, Henry James, and Ford Madox Ford, with whom Conrad collaborated on *The Inheritors* (1901) and *Romance* (1903). It was only after the success of *Chance* (1913), however, that his writing afforded him widespread recognition and relative financial security. He spent his declining years in Kent, often in ill health, and died on August 3, 1924, at his home near Canterbury.

CONTENTS

INTRODUCTION
CARYL PHILLIPS

Joseph Conrad was born Józef Teodor Konrad Korzeniowski in Russian-occupied Poland in 1857. He endured a miserable childhood that was rendered increasingly bleak by the early death of both his parents. The young boy subsequently passed into and out of the care of first one relative and then another, and was subject to much displacement and disruption. This was an era of revolution in which Europe was continually ravaged by war and insurrection, but by the time he was seventeen Conrad had made up his mind to escape both the personal and political turmoil of his homeland. He traveled to Marseilles, where he signed on as a sailor in the merchant marine on a voyage bound for the West Indies and Central America. Conrad soon discovered that there was something reliably soothing about a watery horizon, and he grew to love the solitude of the sea. For the next two decades he voyaged extensively in the Far East, and in Africa and the Americas, his circumnavigations of the globe providing him with opportunities for both education and adventure.

In 1889, a thirty-one year old Conrad chose to settle in London, having three years earlier become a British citizen. He had suffered some maritime hardships, including shipwreck, but he hoped that the many "exotic" countries he had passed through, and the insights he had gleaned about human nature, might form a convincing backdrop for his future writing. In 1890 he traveled again, this time to Belgian Congo, where he kept a detailed diary of his thoughts and observations. When reading it one can sense Conrad the seaman giving way to Conrad the writer. He chose to write in English, although this was his third language after Polish and French, and his first novel, *Almayer's Folly* (1895), met with some success. This encouraged Conrad to henceforth dedicate himself to writing and to effectively turn his back on the peripatetic life of a sailing man.

In 1902 Conrad published his remarkable short novel *Heart of Darkness*, an ironic tale of rescue that contains a powerful meditation on the relationship between "civilization" and "barbarity." Writing in the last month of 1898 and the first month of 1899, Conrad introduces us to five men who are adrift on a "cruising yawl" that rests at anchor on the flooded River Thames to the east of London. As the evening gloom descends, and the fog rolls in, one among them, a strange-looking man named Marlow (the only man among them who still "followed the sea"), begins to narrate the story of a journey he undertook some years earlier into the heart of Africa. A Belgian trading company had commissioned Marlow to take charge of a steamboat and sail up "a mighty big river." Although not at liberty to disclose the full details of his trading mission, it soon transpires that Marlow is expected to discover and, if necessary, rescue a company agent named Kurtz, a brilliant ivory trader who has recently grown silent. As the narrator tells the story of Marlow telling his story—both narratives unfolding simultaneously—the reader experiences the disturbing effect of being seduced up the Congo by spellbinding English prose which evokes a world that is both frightening and fascinating. Conrad's language is high, and impregnated with weighty constructions and rich atmospheric phraseology which teeter on the edge of, but never topple over into, melodrama.

The broadening waters flowed through a mob of wooded islands; you lost your way on that river as you would in a desert, and butted all day long against shoals, trying to find the channel, till you thought yourself bewitched and <u>cut off for ever from everything you had known once</u>—somewhere—<u>far away</u>—in another existence perhaps. There were moments when one's past came back to one, as it will sometimes when you have not a moment to spare to yourself; but it came in the shape of an unrestful and noisy dream, remembered with wonder amongst the overwhelming realities of this strange world of plants, and water, and silence. And this stillness of life did not in the least resemble a peace. It was the stillness of an implacable force brooding over an inscrutable intention. It looked at you with a vengeful aspect.

The ailing Kurtz that Marlow eventually discovers, deep in the heart of the African jungle, is a man who has lost touch with the civilized world. Formerly an artist and sometime journalist, this "African" Kurtz has witnessed, and indulged in, unspecified "barbaric" behavior, and his mind is now mired in delusional megalomania. According to Marlow, "the powers of darkness" have "claimed him for their own." Kurtz bestrides his African "empire," bullying and stealing, yet he is worshiped by the natives as a god, and he is happy to encourage their pagan devotion. Understandably, Kurtz is reluctant to leave his crumbling domain, but Marlow is adamant. He places the dying man aboard his steamboat and begins to take him back to the "real" world, but Kurtz dies en route. At the moment of his death, Kurtz whispers, "The horror! The horror!," a final utterance which addresses the enigmatic heart of the novel. There is the horror of what Kurtz has seen, and there is the horror of Kurtz's realization of his own internal capitulation to savagery; however, for the reader, there is the greater horror of recognizing how quickly the benevolence of European colonization can corrode into European criminality, and how quickly man's capacity for evil can rise from beneath the paper-thin veneer of European "civilization."

One of the great paradoxes of the novel is that while Marlow dislikes Kurtz for having abandoned all decent standards, he also admires this ivory trader for having had the courage to fearlessly explore his "dark" side. Kurtz knew that in order to maintain the imagined harmony of the European world, he would have to master and subdue the chaos of the African world. However, when faced with the reality of the situation, he was unable or unwilling to play one world off against the other, and he submitted to instinct and indulged himself. On returning to Europe, a disturbed Marlow goes out of his way to protect the integrity of Kurtz's decision, and the "truths" that this deceased trader discovered. Through his encounter with Kurtz, Marlow has come to understand that we exist between centuries of darkness and the darkness that will engulf us when we eventually meet our maker. This brief interlude of light is called "life," and it is made possible only by obeying the rules of rank and order. To abandon these rules, like Kurtz, is to pass from darkness to darkness by way of darkness. However, such a miserable and chaotic passage may afford an individual the opportunity to discover "truths" about Man's nature that ordinary mortals, such as Marlow, will fail to perceive.

Written in the wake of the 1884 Berlin Conference, which saw the continent of Africa carved into a "magnificent cake" and divided among European nations, *Heart of Darkness* offered its readers an insight into the "dark" world of Africa. The European world produced the narrator, produced Marlow, and certainly produced the half-French, half-English Kurtz ("All Europe contributed to the making of Kurtz"), but set against the glittering "humanity" of Europe Conrad presents us with a late-nineteenth-century view of a primitive African world that has produced very little, and is clearly doomed to irredeemable savagery. This world picture would have troubled few of Conrad's original readers, for Conrad was merely providing them with the descriptive "evidence" of the bestial people and the fetid world that they "knew" lay beyond Europe. However, by the end of the twentieth century, Conrad's readers are living in a decolonized—indeed postcolonial—world, and Conrad's brutal depiction of African humanity, in order that he might provide a "savage" mirror into which the European might gaze and measure his own tenuous grip on civilization, is now regarded by some readers as problematic.

Among Conrad's more impassioned critics is the Nigerian writer Chinua Achebe, who has little time for Conrad's masterpiece, describing its author as "a bloody racist" and the text as "an offensive and deplorable book." He continues: "… [T]here is a preposterous and perverse kind of arrogance in thus reducing Africa to the role of props for the breakup of one petty European mind." Achebe would appear to be in the camp of those who would submit all literature to the scrutiny of politics, regarding novels and the like as little more than material to be viewed through the prism of empire, colonialism, or some other temporarily fashionable sociocultural construct. This is not to say that the novel is *not* in any way a political form; it is, because like all art it wishes to produce change. However, one cannot judge *Heart of Darkness,* or any novel, on solely political grounds, any more than one can measure the true merit of a politician's speech by employing literary criteria.

Fiction is neither democratic, nor does it respect all points of view, including those that attempt to claim the moral high ground. A reader who fails to recognize that perceptions of race change radically from year to year, and that what appears to be "right on" today can quite easily be perceived of as "unquestionably" reactionary tomorrow, is likely to regard *Heart of Darkness* as "offensive" and Conrad a "racist." In these circumstances how is a writer of fiction, and more specifically the writer of *Heart of Darkness,* supposed to defend himself? Well, the answer is clear. He does not have to, for *Heart of Darkness* is first and foremost a product of its times. It is nonsensical to demand of Conrad that he imagine an African humanity that is totally out of line with both the times in which he was living and the larger purpose of his novel. Even Achebe wistfully concedes that the novel reflects "the dominant image of Africa in the Western imagination." As it happens, the novel does assert European infamy, for there are countless examples throughout the text which point to Conrad's recognition of the illegitimacy of this trading mission and the brutalizing effect it has on the Africans. However, the main focus of the novel is the Europeans and the effect upon them of their encountering another, less "civilized," world. *Heart of Darkness* proposes no program for dismantling European racism or imperialistic exploitation, and the novel should not be confused with an equal opportunity pamphlet. Conrad's only program is doubt; in this case, doubt about the supremacy of European humanity, and the ability of this supposed humanity to maintain its imagined status beyond the high streets of Europe.

There are three remarkable journeys in *Heart of Darkness*. First, Marlow's actual journey upriver to Kurtz's Inner Station. Second, the larger journey that Marlow takes us on from civilized Europe, back to the beginning of creation when nature reigned, and then back to civilized Europe. And finally, the journey that Kurtz undergoes as he sinks down through the many levels of the self to a place where he discovers unlawful and repressed desires. In all three journeys, Conrad explores the multiple ambiguities of civilization, and his restless narrative circles back on itself as though trapped in the complexity of the situation. The overarching question is, what happens when one group of people, supposedly more humane and civilized than another group, attempts to impose themselves upon their "inferiors"? In such circumstances will there always be an individual who, removed from the shackles of "civilized" behavior, feels compelled to push at the margins of conventional "morality"? What happens to this one individual who imagines himself to be released from the moral order of society and therefore free to behave as "savagely" or as "decently" as he deems fit? How does this man respond to chaos?

Conrad uses colonization, and the trading intercourse that flourished in its wake, to explore these universal questions about man's capacity for evil. The end of European colonization has not rendered this *Heart of Darkness* any less relevant, for Conrad is interested in the making of a modern world in which colonization is simply one facet. The uprootedness of people, and their often disquieting encounter with the "other," is a constant theme in his work, and particularly so in this novel. Conrad's writing prepares us for a new world in which modern man has had to endure the psychic and physical pain of displacement, and all the concomitant confusion of watching imagined concrete standards become mutable. Modern descriptions of twentieth-century famines, war, and genocide all seem to be eerily prefigured by Conrad, and *Heart of*

Darkness abounds with passages that seem terrifyingly contemporary in their descriptive accuracy.

> Near the same tree two more bundles of acute angles sat with their legs drawn up. One, with his chin propped on his knees, stared at nothing, in an intolerable and appalling manner: his brother phantom rested its forehead, as if overcome with a great weariness; and all about others were scattered in every pose of contorted collapse, as in some picture of a massacre or a pestilence.

The modern world continues to explode with change and contradiction as past traditions come face-to-face with modern pressure, and modern pressure imposes itself on past traditions. The fissures and fractures of "modernism" are laid bare in this masterwork whose carefully wrought structure creaks under the strain of transition. A supposedly advanced civilization begins to lose its bearings, and "sophisticated" individuals begin to stoop, unable to bear the burden of who they are. To their dismay these individuals discover themselves adrift in situations that challenge their conception of self. They can flee, but the world they will return to will never again seem familiar. Or they can stay and hope to find some kind of resolution to this painful conundrum. Some flee, some stay, but few submit to the confusing confluence of past and present, old and new, with the complete abandonment of a Kurtz, and therefore few discover the "truths" that he does ("The horror! The horror!"). *Heart of Darkness* is peopled with modern men facing new and often terrifying choices. Conrad understood this to be the predicament of our times. Mercifully, most of us will never have to face these questions, but if confronted with our own metaphorical heart of darkness would we have the strength to hold on to the old values while sitting in judgment on the new? Would we have the courage to stare down at "the horror" of whatever it is that lurks in the basement of our modern souls?

———

CARYL PHILLIPS was born in St. Kitts, West Indies, and went with his family to England that same year. He was brought up in Leeds and educated at Oxford. He has written numerous scripts for film, theater, radio, and television. He is the author of one book of nonfiction, *The European Tribe*, and six novels, *The Nature of Blood, The Final Passage, A State of Independence, Higher Ground, Cambridge,* and *Crossing the River*. He is the editor of two anthologies, *Extravagant Strangers: A Literature of Belonging* and *The Right Set: A Tennis Anthology*. Awards he has received include the Martin Luther King Memorial Prize, a Guggenheim Fellowship, and the James Tait Black Memorial Prize. He divides his time between London and New York City.

COMMENTARY

BY

H. L. MENCKEN

E. M. FORSTER

VIRGINIA WOOLF

ERNEST HEMINGWAY

BERTRAND RUSSELL

LIONEL TRILLING

CHINUA ACHEBE

PHILIP GOUREVITCH

H. L. MENCKEN

Like Dreiser, Conrad is forever fascinated by the "immense indifference of things," the tragic vanity of the blind groping that we call aspiration, the profound meaninglessness of life—fascinated, and left wondering. One looks in vain for an attempt at a solution of the riddle in the whole canon of his work. Dreiser, more than once, seems ready to take refuge behind an indeterminate sort of mysticism, even a facile supernaturalism, but Conrad, from first to last, faces squarely the massive and intolerable fact. His stories are not chronicles of men who conquer fate, nor of men who are unbent and undaunted by fate, but of men who are conquered and undone. Each protagonist is a new Prometheus, with a sardonic ignominy piled upon his helplessness. Each goes down a Greek route to defeat and disaster, leaving nothing behind him save an unanswered question. I can scarcely recall an exception. Kurtz, Lord Jim, Razumov, Nostromo, Captain Whalley, Yanko Goorall, Verloc, Heyst, Gaspar Ruiz, Almayer: one and all they are destroyed and made a mock of by the blind, incomprehensible forces that beset them.

—

Conrad . . . grounds his work firmly upon [a] sense of cosmic implacability, [a] confession of unintelligibility. The exact point of the story of Kurtz, in "Heart of Darkness," is that it is pointless, that Kurtz's death is as meaningless as his life, that the moral of such a sordid tragedy is a wholesale negation of all morals. . . .

[Conrad] brings into the English fiction of the day, not only an artistry that is vastly more fluent and delicate than the general, but also a highly unusual sophistication, a quite extraordinary detachment from all petty rages and puerile certainties. The winds of doctrine, howling all about him, leave him absolutely unmoved. He belongs to no party and has nothing to teach, save only a mystery as old as man. In the midst of the hysterical splutterings and battle-cries of the Kiplings and Chestertons, the booming pedagogics of the Wellses and Shaws, and the smirking at keyholes of the Bennetts and de Morgans, he stands apart and almost alone, observing the sardonic comedy of man with an eye that sees every point and significance of it, but vouchsafing none of that sophomoric indignation, that Hyde Park wisdom, that flabby moralizing which freight and swamp the modern English novel. "At the centre of his web," says Arthur Symons [in *Forum*, May 1915] "sits an elemental sarcasm discussing human affairs with a calm and cynical ferocity. . . . He calls up all the dreams and illusions by which men have been destroyed and saved, and lays them mockingly naked. . . . He shows the bare side of every virtue, the hidden heroism of every vice and crime. He summons before him all the injustices that have come to birth out of ignorance and self-love. . . . And in all this there is no judgment, only an implacable comprehension, as of one outside nature, to whom joy and sorrow, right and wrong, savagery and civilization, are equal and indifferent. . . ."

Obviously, no Englishman! No need to explain (with something akin to apology) that his name is really not Joseph Conrad at all, but Teodor Josef Konrad Karzeniowski, and that he is a Pole of noble lineage, with a vague touch of the Asiatic in him. The Anglo-Saxon mind, in these later days, becomes increasingly incapable of his whole point of view. Put into plain language, his doctrine can only fill it with wonder and fury. That mind is essentially moral in cut; it is believing, certain, indignant; it is as incapable of skepticism, save as a passing coryza of the spirit, as it is of wit, which is skepticism's daughter. Time was when this was not true, as Congreve, Pope, Wycherley and even Thackeray show, but that time was before the Reform Bill of 1832, the great intellectual levelling, the emancipation of the *chandala*. In these our days the Englishman is an incurable foe of distinction, and being so he must needs take in with his mother's milk the delusions which go with that enmity, and particularly the master delusion that all human problems, in the last analysis, are readily soluble, and that all that is required for their solution is to take counsel freely, to listen to wizards, to count votes, to agree upon legislation. ...

My business, however, is not with the culture of Anglo-Saxondom, but only with Conrad's place therein. That place is isolated and remote; he is neither of it nor quite in it. In the midst of a futile meliorism which deceives the more, the more it soothes, he stands out like some sinister skeleton at the feast, regarding the festivities with a flickering and impenetrable grin. "To read him," says Arthur Symons, "is to shudder on the edge of a gulf, in a silent darkness." There is no need to be told that he is there almost by accident, that he came in a chance passerby, a bit uncertain of the door. It was not an artistic choice that made him write English instead of French; it was a choice with its roots in considerations far afield. But once made, it concerned him no further. In his first book he was plainly a stranger, and all himself; in his last he is a stranger still—strange in his manner of speech, strange in his view of life, strange, above all, in his glowing and gorgeous artistry, his enthusiasm for beauty *per se*, his absolute detachment from that heresy which would make it no more than a servant to some bald and depressing theory of conduct, some axiom of the uncomprehending. He is, like Dunsany, a pure artist. His work, as he once explained, is not to edify, to console, to improve or to encourage, but simply to get upon paper some shadow of his own eager sense of the wonder and prodigality of life as men live it in the world, and of its unfathomable romance and mystery. "My task," he went on [in *The New Review*, December 1897], "is, by the power of the written word, to make you hear, to make you feel—it is, before all, to make you *see*. That—and no more, and it is everything." ...

This detachment from all infra-and-ultra-artistic purpose, this repudiation of the rôle of propagandist, this avowal of what Nietzsche was fond of calling innocence, explains the failure of Conrad to fit into the pigeon-holes so laboriously prepared for him by critics who must shelve and label or be damned. He is too big for any of them, and of a shape too strange. He stands clear, not only of all the schools and factions that obtain in latter-day English fiction, but also of the whole stream of English literature since the Restoration. He is as isolated a figure as George Moore, and for much the same reason. Both are exotics, and both, in a very real sense, are public enemies, for both war upon the philosophies that caress the herd.... [Conrad] is not only a finer artist than Kipling; he is a quite different kind of artist. Kipling, within his limits, shows a talent of a very high order. He is a craftsman of the utmost deftness. He gets his effects with almost perfect assurance. Moreover, there is a poet in him; he knows how to reach the emotions. But once his stories are stripped down to the bare carcass their emptiness becomes immediately apparent. The ideas in them are not the ideas of a reflective and perspicacious man, but simply the ideas of a mob-orator, a mouther of inanities, a bugler, a schoolgirl. Reduce any of them to a simple proposition, and that proposition, in so far as it is intelligible at all, will be ridiculous. It is precisely here that Conrad leaps immeasurably ahead. His ideas are not only sound; they are acute and unusual. They plough down into the sub-strata of human motive and act. They unearth conditions and considerations that lie concealed from the superficial glance. They get at the primary reactions. In particular and above all, they combat the conception of man as a pet and privy councillor of the gods, working out his own destiny in a sort of vacuum and constantly illumined by infallible revelations of his duty, and expose him as he is in fact: an organism infinitely more sensitive and responsive than other organisms, but still a mere organism in the end, a brother to the wild things and the protozoa, swayed by the same inscrutable fortunes, condemned to the same inchoate errors and irresolutions, and surrounded by the same terror and darkness....

But is the Conrad I here describe simply a new variety of moralist, differing from the general only in the drift of the doctrine he preaches? Surely not. He is no more a moralist than an atheist is a theologian. His attitude toward all moral systems and axioms is that of a skeptic who rejects them unanimously, even including, and perhaps especially including, those to which, in moments of æsthetic detachment, he seems to give a formal and resigned sort of assent. It is this constant falling back upon "I do not know," this incessant conversion of the easy logic of romance into the harsh and dismaying logic of fact, that explains his failure to succeed as a popular novelist, despite his skill at evoking emotion, his towering artistic passion, his power to tell a thumping tale. He is talked of, he brings forth a mass of punditic criticism, he becomes in a sense the fashion; but it would be absurd to say that he has made the same profound impression upon the great class of normal novel-readers that Arnold Bennett once made, or H. G. Wells, or William de Morgan in his brief day, or even such cheap-jacks as Anthony Hope Hawkins and William J. Locke. His show fascinates, but his philosophy, in the last analysis, is unbearable. . . .

———

As for Conrad the literary craftsman, opposing him for the moment to Conrad the showman of the human comedy, the quality that all who write about him seem chiefly to mark in him is his scorn of conventional form, his tendency to approach his story from two directions at once, his frequent involvement in apparently inextricable snarls of narrative, sub-narrative and sub-sub-narrative. . . .

The Kipling-Wells style of swift, shouldering, button-holing writing has accustomed readers and critics alike to a straight course and a rapid tempo. Moreover, it has accustomed them to a forthright certainty and directness of statement; they expect an author to account for his characters at once, and on grounds instantly comprehensible. This omniscience is a part of the prodigality of moral theory that I have been discussing. An author who knows just what is the matter with the world may be quite reasonably expected to know just what is the matter with his hero. Neither sort of assurance, I need not say, is to be found in Conrad. He is an inquirer, not a law-giver; an experimentalist, not a doctor. One constantly derives from his stories the notion that he is as much puzzled by his characters as the reader is—that he, too, is feeling his way among shadowy evidences. The discoveries that we make, about Lord Jim, about Nostromo or about Kurtz, come as fortuitously and as unexpectedly as the discoveries we make about the real figures of our world. The picture is built up bit by bit; it is never flashed suddenly and completely as by best-seller calciums; it remains a bit dim at the end. But in that very dimness, so tantalizing and yet so revealing, lies two-thirds of Conrad's art, or his craft, or his trick, or whatever you choose to call it. What he shows us is blurred at the edges, but so is life itself blurred at the edges. We see least clearly precisely what is nearest to us, and is hence most real to us. A man may profess to understand the President of the United States, but he seldom alleges, even to himself, that he understands his own wife.

In the character and in its reactions, in the act and in the motive: always that tremulousness, that groping, that confession of final bewilderment. "He passes away under a cloud, inscrutable at heart...." And the cloud enshrouds the inner man as well as the outer, the secret springs of his being as well as the overt events of his life. "His meanest creatures," says Arthur Symons, "have in them a touch of honour, of honesty, or of heroism; his heroes have always some error, weakness, or mistake, some sin or crime, to redeem." What is Lord Jim, scoundrel and poltroon or gallant knight? What is Captain MacWhirr, hero or simply ass? What is Falk, beast or idealist? One leaves "Heart of Darkness" in that palpitating confusion which is shot through with intense curiosity. Kurtz is at once the most abominable of rogues and the most fantastic of dreamers. It is impossible to differentiate between his vision and his crimes, though all that we look upon as order in the universe stands between them. In Dreiser's novels there is the same anarchy of valuations, and it is chiefly responsible for the rage he excites in the unintelligent. The essential thing about Cowperwood is that he is two diverse beings at once; a puerile chaser of women and a great artist, a guinea pig and half a god. The essential thing about Carrie Meeber is that she remains innocent in the midst of her contaminations, that the virgin lives on in the kept woman. This is not the art of fiction as it is conventionally practised and understood. It is not explanation, labelling, assurance, moralizing. In the cant of newspaper criticism, it does not "satisfy." But the great artist is never one who satisfies in that feeble sense; he leaves the business to mountebanks who do it better. "My purpose," said Ibsen, "is not to answer questions; it is to ask them." The spectator must bring something with him beyond the mere faculty of attention. If, coming to Conrad, he cannot, he is at the wrong door.

———

Conrad's predilection for barbarous scenes and the more bald and shocking sort of drama has an obviously autobiographical basis. His own road ran into strange places in the days of his youth. He moved among men who were menaced by all the terrestrial cruelties, and by the almost unchecked rivalry and rapacity of their fellow men, without any appreciable barriers, whether of law, of convention or of sentimentality, to shield them. The struggle for existence, as he saw it, was well nigh as purely physical among human beings as among the carnivora of the jungle. Some of his stories, and among them his very best, are plainly little more than transcripts of his own experience. He himself is the enchanted boy of "Youth"; he is the ship-master of "Heart of Darkness"; he hovers in the background of all the island books and is visibly present in most of the tales of the sea.

And what he got out of that early experience was more than a mere body of reminiscence; it was a scheme of valuations. He came to his writing years with a sailor's disdain for the trifling hazards and emprises of market places and drawing rooms, and it shows itself whenever he sets pen to paper. A conflict, it would seem, can make no impression upon him save it be colossal. When his men combat, not nature, but other men, they carry over into the business the gigantic method of sailors battling with a tempest. "The Secret Agent" and "Under Western Eyes" fill the dull back streets of London and Geneva with pursuits, homicides and dynamitings. "Nostromo" is a long record of treacheries, butcheries and carnalities. "A Point of Honor" is coloured by the senseless, insatiable ferocity of Gobineau's "Renaissance." "Victory" ends with a massacre of all the chief personages, a veritable catastrophe of blood. Whenever he turns from the starker lusts to the pale passions of man under civilization, Conrad fails. "The Return" is a thoroughly infirm piece of writing—a second rate magazine story. One concludes at once that the author himself does not believe in it. "The Inheritors" is worse; it becomes, after the first few pages, a flaccid artificiality, a bore. It is impossible to imagine the chief characters of the Conrad gallery in such scenes. Think of Captain MacWhirr reacting to social tradition, Lord Jim immersed in the class war, Lena Hermann seduced by the fashions, Almayer a candidate for office! As well think of Huckleberry Finn at Harvard, or Tom Jones practising law.

These things do not interest Conrad, chiefly, I suppose, because he does not understand them. His concern, one may say, is with the gross anatomy of passion, not with its histology. He seeks to depict emotion, not in its ultimate attenuation, but in its fundamental innocence and fury. Inevitably, his materials are those of what we call melodrama; he is at one, in the bare substance of his tales, with the manufacturers of the baldest shockers. But with a difference!—a difference, to wit, of approach and comprehension, a difference abysmal and revolutionary. He lifts melodrama to the dignity of an important business, and makes it a means to an end that the mere shock-monger never dreams of. In itself, remember, all this up-roar and blood-letting is not incredible, nor even improbable. The world, for all the pressure of order, is still full of savage and stupendous conflicts, of murders and debaucheries, of crimes indescribable and adventures almost unimaginable. One cannot reasonably ask a novelist to deny them or to gloss over them; all one may demand of him is that, if he make artistic use of them, he render them understandable—that he logically account for them, that he give them plausibility by showing their genesis in intelligible motives and colourable events. . . .

The true answer, when it is forthcoming at all, is always much more complex than the melodramatist's answer. It may be so enormously complex, indeed, as to transcend all the normal laws of cause and effect. It may be an answer made up largely, or even wholly, of the fantastic, the astounding, the unearthly reasons of lunacy. That is the chief, if not the only difference between melodrama and reality. The events of the two may be, and often are identical. It is only in their underlying network of causes that they are dissimilar and incommensurate.

Here, in brief, you have the point of essential distinction between the stories of Conrad, a supreme artist in fiction, and the trashy confections of the literary artisans—*e.g.,* Sienkiewicz, Dumas, Lew Wallace, and their kind. Conrad's materials, at bottom, are almost identical with those of the artisans. He, too, has his chariot races, his castaways, his carnivals of blood in the arena. He, too, takes us through shipwrecks, revolutions, assassinations, gaudy heroisms, abominable treacheries. But always he illuminates the nude and amazing event with shafts of light which reveal not only the last detail of its workings, but also the complex of origins and inducements behind it. Always, he throws about it a probability which, in the end, becomes almost inevitability. . . .

In all his stories you will find [a] . . . concern with the inextricable movement of phenomena and noumena between event and event, this same curiosity as to first causes and ultimate effects. Sometimes, as in "The Point of Honor" and "The End of the Tether," he attempts to work out the obscure genesis, in some chance emotion or experience, of an extraordinary series of transactions. At other times, as in "Typhoon," "Youth," "Falk" and "The Shadow Line," his endeavour is to determine the effect of some gigantic and fortuitous event upon the mind and soul of a given man. At yet other times, as in "Almayer's Folly," "Lord Jim" and "Under Western Eyes," it is his aim to show how cause and effect are intricately commingled, so that it is difficult to separate motive from consequence, and consequence from motive. But always it is the process of mind rather than the actual act that interests him. Always he is trying to penetrate the actor's mask and interpret the actor's frenzy. It is this concern with the profounder aspects of human nature, this bold grappling with the deeper and more recondite problems of his art, that gives him consideration as a first-rate artist. He differs from the common novelists of his time as a Beethoven differs from a Mendelssohn. Some of them are quite his equals in technical skill, and a few of them, notably Bennett and Wells, often show an actual superiority, but when it comes to that graver business which underlies all mere virtuosity, he is unmistakably the superior of the whole corps of them.

This superiority is only the more vividly revealed by the shopworn shoddiness of most of his materials. He takes whatever is nearest to hand, out of his own rich experience or out of the common store of romance. He seems to disdain the petty advantages which go with the invention of novel plots, extravagant characters and unprecedented snarls of circumstance. All the classical doings of anarchists are to be found in "The Secret Agent"; one has heard them copiously credited, of late, to so-called Reds. "Youth," as a story, is no more than an orthodox sea story, and W. Clark Russell contrived better ones. In "Chance" we have a stern father at his immemorial tricks. In "Victory" there are villains worthy of Jack B. Yeats' melodramas of the Spanish Main. In "Nostromo" we encounter the whole stock company of Richard Harding Davis and O. Henry. And in "Under Western Eyes" the protagonist is one who finds his love among the women of his enemies—a situation at the heart of all the military melodramas ever written.

But what Conrad makes of that ancient and flyblown stuff, that rubbish from the lumber room of the imagination! Consider, for example, "Under Western Eyes," by no means the best of his stories. The plot is that of "Shenandoah" and "Held by the Enemy"—but how brilliantly it is endowed with a new significance, how penetratingly its remotest currents are followed out, how magnificently it is made to fit into that colossal panorama of Holy Russia! It is always this background, this complex of obscure and baffling influences, this drama under the drama, that Conrad spends his skill upon, and not the obvious commerce of the actual stage. It is not the special effect that he seeks, but the general effect. It is not so much man the individual that interests him, as the shadowy accumulation of traditions, instincts and blind chances which shapes the individual's destiny. Here, true enough, we have a full-length portrait of Razumov, glowing with life. But here, far more importantly, we also have an amazingly meticulous and illuminating study of the Russian character, with all its confused mingling of Western realism and Oriental fogginess, its crazy tendency to go shooting off into the spaces of an incomprehensible metaphysic, its general transcendence of all that we Celts and Saxons and Latins hold to be true of human motive and human act. Russia is a world apart: that is the sum and substance of the tale. In the island stories we have the same elaborate projection of the East, of its fantastic barbarism, of brooding Asia. And in the sea stories we have, perhaps for the first time in English fiction, a vast and adequate picture of the sea, the symbol at once of man's eternal striving and of his eternal impotence. Here, at last, the colossus has found its interpreter. There is in "Typhoon" and "The Nigger of the Narcissus," and, above all, in "The Mirror of the Sea," a poetic evocation of the sea's stupendous majesty that is unparalleled outside the ancient sagas. Conrad describes it with a degree of graphic skill that is superb and incomparable. He challenges at once the pictorial vigour of Hugo and the aesthetic sensitiveness of Lafcadio Hearn, and surpasses them both. And beyond this mere dazzling visualization, he gets into his pictures an overwhelming sense of that vast drama of which they are no more than the flat, lifeless representation—of that inexorable and uncompassionate struggle which is life itself. The sea to him is a living thing, an omnipotent and unfathomable thing, almost a god. He sees it as the Eternal Enemy, deceitful in its caresses, sudden in its rages, relentless in its enmities, and forever a mystery.

———

Conrad's first novel, "Almayer's Folly," was printed in 1895. He tells us in "A Personal Record" that it took him seven years to write it—seven years of pertinacious effort, of trial and error, of learning how to write. He was, at this time thirty-eight years old. Seventeen years before, landing in England to fit himself for the British merchant service, he had made his first acquaintance with the English language. The interval had been spent almost continuously at sea—in the Eastern islands, along the China coast, on the Congo and in the South Atlantic. That he hesitated between French and English is a story often told, but he himself is authority for the statement that it is more symbolical than true. Flaubert, in those days, was his idol, as we know, but the speech of his daily business won, and English literature reaped the greatest of all its usufructs from English sea power. To this day there are marks of his origins in his style. His periods, more than once, have an inept and foreign smack. In fishing for the right phrase one sometimes feels that he finds a French phrase, or even a Polish phrase, and that it loses something by being done into English. . . .

—

There is a notion that judgments of living artists are impossible. They are bound to be corrupted, we are told, by prejudice, false perspective, mob emotion, error. The question whether this or that man is great or small is one which only posterity can answer. A silly begging of the question, for doesn't posterity also make mistakes? Shakespeare's ghost has seen two or three posterities, beautifully at odds. Even today, it must notice a difference in flitting from London to Berlin. The shade of Milton has been tricked in the same way. So, also, has Johann Sebastian Bach's. It needed a Mendelssohn to rescue it from Coventry—and now Mendelssohn himself, once so shining a light, is condemned to the shadows in his turn. We are not dead yet; we are here, and it is now. Therefore, let us at least venture, guess, opine.

My own conviction, sweeping all those reaches of living fiction that I know, is that Conrad's figure stands out from the field like the Alps from the Piedmont plain. He not only has no masters in the novel; he has scarcely a colourable peer. Perhaps Thomas Hardy and Anatole France—old men both, their work behind them. But who else? James is dead. Meredith is dead. So is George Moore, though he lingers on. So are all the Russians of the first rank; Andrieff, Gorki and their like are light cavalry. In Sudermann, Germany has a writer of short stories of very high calibre, but where is the German novelist to match Conrad? Clara Viebig? Thomas Mann? Gustav Frenssen? Arthur Schnitzler? Surely not! As for the Italians, they are either absurd tear-squeezers or more absurd harlequins. As for the Spaniards and the Scandinavians, they would pass for geniuses only in Suburbia. In America, setting aside an odd volume here and there, one can discern only Dreiser. . . . There remains England. England has the best second-raters in the world; nowhere else is the general level of novel writing so high; nowhere else is there a corps of journeyman novelists comparable to Wells, Bennett, Benson, Walpole, Beresford, George, Galsworthy, Hichens, De Morgan,

Miss Sinclair, Hewlett and company. They have a prodigious facility; they know how to write; even the least of them is, at all events, a more competent artisan than, say, Dickens, or Bulwer-Lytton, or Sienkiewicz, or Zola. But the literary *grande passion* is simply not in them. They get nowhere with their suave and interminable volumes. Their view of the world and its wonders is narrow and superficial. They are, at bottom, no more than clever mechanicians.

As Galsworthy has said, Conrad lifts himself immeasurably above them all. One might well call him, if the term had not been cheapened into cant, a cosmic artist. His mind works upon a colossal scale; he conjures up the general out of the particular. What he sees and describes in his books is not merely this man's aspiration or that woman's destiny, but the overwhelming sweep and devastation of universal forces, the great central drama that is at the heart of all other dramas, the tragic struggles of the soul of man under the gross stupidity and obscene joking of the gods. "In the novels of Conrad," says Galsworthy, "nature is first, man is second." But not a mute, a docile second! He may think, as Walpole argues, that "life is too strong, too clever and too remorseless for the sons of men," but he does not think that they are too weak and poor in spirit to challenge it. It is the challenging that engrosses him, and enchants him, and raises up the magic of his wonder. It is as futile, in the end, as Hamlet's or Faust's—but still a gallant and a gorgeous adventure, a game uproariously worth the playing, an enterprise "inscrutable... and excessively romantic."...

If you want to get his measure, read "Youth" or "Falk" or "Heart of Darkness," and then try to read the best of Kipling. I think you will come to some understanding, by that simple experiment, of the difference between an adroit artisan's bag of tricks and the lofty sincerity and passion of a first-rate artist.

From "Joseph Conrad," *A Book of Prefaces*, 1917

E. M. FORSTER

[The essays composing Conrad's *Notes on Life and Letters*] suggest that he is misty in the middle as well as at the edges, that the secret casket of his genius contains a vapour rather than a jewel; and that we need not try to write him down philosophically, because there is, in this particular direction, nothing to write. No creed, in fact. Only opinions, and the right to throw them overboard when facts make them look absurd. Opinions held under the semblance of eternity ... and therefore easily mistaken for a creed.

As the simple sailorman, concerned only with his job, and resenting interference, he is not difficult to understand, and it is this side of him that has given what is most solid, though not what is most splendid, to his books. ...

He has no respect for adventure, unless it comes incidentally. If pursued for its own sake it leads to "red noses and watery eyes," and "lays a man under no obligation of faithfulness to an idea." Work filled the life of the men whom he admired and imitated and whom, more articulate than they, he would express. ...

He does not respect all humanity. Indeed, were he less self-conscious, he would probably be a misanthrope. He has to pull himself up with a reminder that misanthropy wouldn't be quite fair—on himself. ... It becomes a point of honour not to be misanthropic, so that even when he hits out there is a fierce restraint that wounds more deeply than the blows. He will not despise men, yet cannot respect them, and consequently our careers seem to him important and unimportant at the same time, and our fates, like those of the characters of Alphonse Daudet, "poignant, intensely interesting, and not of the slightest consequence."

Now, together with these loyalties and prejudices and personal scruples, he holds another ideal, a universal, the love of Truth. But Truth is a flower in whose neighbourhood others must wither, and Mr. Conrad has no intention that the blossoms he has culled with such pains and in so many lands should suffer and be thrown aside. So there are constant discrepancies between his nearer and his further vision, and here would seem to be the cause of his central obscurity. If he lived only in his experiences, never lifting his eyes to what lies beyond them: or if, having seen what lies beyond, he would subordinate his experiences to it—then in either case he would be easier to read. But he is in neither case. He is too much of a seer to restrain his spirit; he is too much Joseph Conrad, too jealous of personal honour, to give any but the fullest value to deeds and dangers he has known.

Neither explicitly nor implicitly does Mr. Conrad demand friendship: he desires no good wishes from his readers: the anonymous intimacy, so dear to most, is only an annoyance and a hindrance to him.

From "Joseph Conrad: A Note" (1920) in *Albinger Harvest*, 1936

VIRGINIA WOOLF

There is nothing colloquial in Conrad; nothing intimate; and no humour, at least of the English kind. And those are great drawbacks for a novelist, you will admit. Then, of course, it goes without saying that he is a romantic. No one objects to that. But it entails a terrible penalty—death at the age of forty—death or disillusionment. If your romantic persists in living, he must face his disillusionment. He must make his music out of contrasts. But Conrad has never faced his disillusionment. He goes on singing the same songs about sea captains and the sea, beautiful, noble, and monotonous; but now I think with a crack in the flawless strain of his youth. It is a mind of one fact; and such a mind can never be among the classics. . . .

My theory is made of cobwebs, no doubt . . . [but] of this I am certain. Conrad is not one and simple; no, he is many and complex. . . . And Mr. Conrad's selves are particularly opposite. He is composed of two people who have nothing whatever in common. He is your sea captain, simple, faithful, obscure; and he is Marlow, subtle, psychological, loquacious. In the early books the Captain dominates; in the later it is Marlow at least who does all the talking. The union of these two very different men makes for all sorts of queer effects. You must have noticed the sudden silences, the awkward collisions, the immense lethargy which threatens at every moment to descend. All this, I think, must be the result of that internal conflict. . . . In Conrad's novels personal relations are never final. Men are tested by their attitude to august abstractions. Are they faithful, are they honourable, are they courageous? The men he loves are reserved for death in the bosom of the sea. . . .

He sees once and he sees for ever. His books are full of moments of vision. They light up a whole character in a flash. . . . The beauty of surface has always a fibre of morality within. I seem to see each of the sentences . . . advancing with resolute bearing and a calm which they have won in strenuous conflict, against the forces of falsehood, sentimentality, and slovenliness. He could not write badly, one feels, to save his life.

From "Mr. Conrad: A Conversation" (1923) in
The Captain's Death Bed and Other Essays, 1950

ERNEST HEMINGWAY

It is fashionable among my friends to disparage [Conrad]. It is even necessary. Living in a world of literary politics where one wrong opinion often proves fatal, one writes carefully. . . .

It is agreed by most of the people I know that Conrad is a bad writer, just as it is agreed that T. S. Eliot is a good writer. If I knew that by grinding Mr. Eliot into a fine dry powder and sprinkling that powder over Mr. Conrad's grave Mr. Conrad would shortly appear, looking very annoyed at the forced return, and commence writing I would leave for London early tomorrow morning with a sausage grinder. . . .

The second book of Conrad's that I read was *Lord Jim*. I was unable to finish it. It is, therefore, all I have left of him. For I cannot re-read them. That may be what my friends mean by saying he is a bad writer. But from nothing else that I have ever read have I gotten what every book of Conrad has given me.

Knowing I could not re-read them I saved up four that I would not read until I needed them badly, when the disgust with writing, writers and everything written of and to write would be too much. Two months in Toronto used up the four books. . . .

In Sudbury, Ontario, I bought three back numbers of the *Pictorial Review* and read *The Rover*, sitting up in bed in the Nickle Range Hotel. When morning came I had used up all my Conrad like a drunkard, I had hoped it would last me the trip, and felt like a young man who has blown his patrimony. But, I thought, he will write more stories. He has lots of time.

When I read the reviews they all agreed *The Rover* was a bad story.

And now he is dead and I wish to God they would have taken some great, acknowledged technician of a literary figure and left him to write his bad stories.

From "Conrad, Optimist and Moralist," *Transatlantic Review,*
October 1924

BERTRAND RUSSELL

Of all that he had written I admired most the terrible story called *The Heart of Darkness*, in which a rather weak idealist is driven mad by horror of the tropical forest and loneliness among savages. This story expresses, I think, most completely his philosophy of life. I felt, though I do not know whether he would have accepted such an image, that he thought of civilized and morally tolerable human life as a dangerous walk on a thin crust of barely cooled lava which at any moment might break and let the unwary sink into fiery depths. He was very conscious of the various forms of passionate madness to which men are prone, and it was this that gave him such a profound belief in the importance of discipline.

From "Joseph Conrad" in *Portraits from Memory and Other Essays*, 1956

LIONEL TRILLING

What I take to be the paradigmatic literary expression of the modern concern with authenticity is Joseph Conrad's great short novel *Heart of Darkness*, which appeared, with some appropriateness, in the next to the last year of the nineteenth century. This troubling work has no manifest polemical intention but it contains in sum the whole of the radical critique of European civilization that has been made by literature in the years since its publication.

In several respects the story has a striking affinity with Diderot's *Neveu de Rameau*. A man of unimpeachable moral character, a sensitive and reflective man but not inclined to raise radical questions about life, in short, an "honest soul," a Diderot-*Moi*, is brought into confrontation with a *Lui*, who, however, is not a wild genius of cynicism like Diderot's Rameau but a man whose foul and bloody deeds make him what the terms of the story permit us to call a devil. Yet Marlow, the "honest soul" who narrates the story, accords Kurtz an admiration and loyalty which amount to homage, and not, it would seem, in spite of his deeds but because of them.

As with Diderot's Rameau, it is scarcely possible to describe the character of Kurtz at once summarily and accurately. It is of the essence of his fate that Kurtz is implicated in one of the most brazen political insincerities ever perpetrated. The Berlin Congress, convened by Bismarck in 1885, established the King of the Belgians, Leopold II, in personal possession of and sovereignty over the so-called Congo Free State. Leopold's rule, through his surrogates, was absolute and ruthless, carried out with monstrous cruelty, but the royal Tartuffe had no difficulty in convincing the world that he was doing the work of civilization, bringing light to the brothers who sat in darkness. Marlow has no sooner set foot in the Congo than he perceives and is revolted by the discrepancy between these avowals of beneficent purpose and the terrible actuality of heartless oppression. But Kurtz, who is an agent of one of the great Belgian trading companies, at least for a time carries on his work in the belief that he is opening the country not only to trade but to the light that shines from Europe, and there is no clear indication in the story that he ever recognizes, let alone repudiates, the vast hypocrisy his nation is practising.

To the making of Kurtz, we are told, all Europe has contributed: the nationality of his parents is mixed; he is an amateur, more or less gifted, of the high arts, a writer, a painter, a musician; he professes the rational altruistic ethic of educated Europeans of good will. Marlow first hears of him as a man of superior intellectual and moral qualities which isolate him from his colleagues and make him the object of their envy and spite. The stunning *peripeteia* of the story is the revelation that Kurtz, having gone alone to collect ivory far up the Congo River, has become the chief and virtually the god of a local tribe, his rule being remarkable for its cruelty.

Kurtz, it must be clear, did not choose the life of savagery out of any sentimental illusion that it is noble and virtuous. On the contrary, he is appalled by it—one of his high-minded reports on the natives which Marlow reads after his death breaks off suddenly with the scrawl, "Exterminate all the brutes!" And Marlow himself, although on one occasion he feels the frightening fascination of the savage life, allows it none of the charm that anthropologists commonly discover in tribal ways; he cannot withhold admiration from the manly grace of the natives but he looks upon the culture that bred them as sordid and terrible, in its own fashion as evil as the European culture which oppresses it. His word for it is Biblical and conclusive: it is the "abomination." Nor does Marlow suggest that Kurtz, by embracing savagery, has found redemption in any personal moral sense: he has purged himself of none of the European vices, not even greed. For Marlow, nevertheless, Kurtz is a hero of the spirit whom he cherishes as Theseus at Colonus cherished

Oedipus: he sinned for all mankind. By his regression to savagery Kurtz had reached as far down beneath the constructs of civilization as it was possible to go, to the irreducible truth of man, the innermost core of his nature, his heart of darkness. From that Stygian authenticity comes illumination, the light cast not only on the souls of the Belgian business agents, servants of what Marlow calls a "flabby, pretending, weak-eyed devil," but also on the soul of Kurtz's dedicated fiancée, who embodies all the self-cherishing, self-deceiving idealism of Europe, that noble "Intended," monumental in her bereavement, appalling to Marlow in her certitude that her lost lover had been the reproachless knight of altruism.

But if, by this light, Marlow sees civilization as fraudulent and shameful, we yet confront the paradox that at the same time he has a passionate commitment to civilization, just so it is the right sort. Which is to say, just so it is English. The brilliant scene with which the story opens is set on a cruising yawl in the estuary of the Thames and is in effect a hymn, in which Marlow and the primary narrator join their voices, to the Englishness of the river. The aspect it would have had for the colonizing Romans is conjured up—no less primordially dark, inscrutable, threatening than the Congo seems to nineteenth-century Europeans. With the passing of the centuries, however, the English river has become an object of veneration for good men, who see it "in the august light of abiding memories." And the Thames has its own light, it is a source of light to the world: "Light came from this river." The great adventurers and settlers have sailed out from it—Marlow speaks of them as "bearers of a spark from the sacred fire." They carried to distant lands "the seeds of commonwealth," and, not least of England's beneficences, "the germ of empire." To be sure, adventurers had set out from other lands too; we are to hear, later in the story, of the French, the Germans, and of course much of the Belgians. But they were wholly unlike the English. "These chaps were not much account really," says Marlow. "They were conquerors, and for that you want only brute force.... They grabbed what they could for the sake of what was in it.... It was just robbery with violence...." And he goes on: "The conquest of the earth, which mostly means the taking it away from those who have a different complexion or slightly flatter noses than ourselves, is not a pretty thing when you look at it too much. What redeems it is the idea only. An idea at the back of it; not a sentimental pretence but an idea; and an unselfish belief in the idea—something you can set up, and bow down before, and offer a sacrifice to." Marlow does not doubt that it is the English alone who have such an idea.

Heart of Darkness, then, is a story that strangely moves in two quite opposite directions—on the one hand, to the view that civilization is of its nature so inauthentic that personal integrity can be wrested from it only by the inversion of all its avowed principles; on the other hand, to the categorical assertion that civilization can and does fulfil its announced purposes, not universally, indeed, but at least in the significant instance of one particular nation.

From "Society and Authenticity," in *Sincerity and Authenticity,* 1971

CHINUA ACHEBE

[It] is the desire—one might indeed say the need—in Western psychology to set Africa up as a foil to Europe, a place of negations at once remote and vaguely familiar in comparison with which Europe's own state of spiritual grace will be manifest. . . .

Joseph Conrad's *Heart of Darkness* . . . better than any other work that I know displays that Western desire and need. . . . Of course, there are whole libraries of books devoted to the same purpose, but most of them are so obvious and so crude that few people worry about them today. Conrad, on the other hand, is undoubtedly one of the great stylists of modern fiction and a good storyteller in the bargain. His contribution, therefore, falls automatically into a different class—permanent literature—read and taught and constantly evaluated by serious academics. *Heart of Darkness* is indeed so secure today that a leading Conrad scholar has numbered it "among the half-dozen greatest short novels in the English language.". . .

Heart of Darkness projects the image of Africa as "the other world," the antithesis of Europe and therefore of civilization, a place where man's vaunted intelligence and refinement are finally mocked by triumphant bestiality. The book opens on the River Thames, tranquil, resting peacefully "at the decline of day after ages of good service done to the race that peopled its banks." But the actual story takes place on the River Congo, the very antithesis of the Thames. The River Congo is quite decidedly not a River Emeritus. It has rendered no service and enjoys no old-age pension. We are told that "going up that river was like travelling back to the earliest beginnings of the world."

Is Conrad saying, then, that these two rivers are very different, one good, the other bad? Yes, but that is not the real point. It is not the differentness that worries Conrad but the lurking hint of kinship, of common ancestry. For the Thames too "has been one of the dark places of the earth." It conquered its darkness, of course, and is now at peace. But if it were to visit its primordial relative, the Congo, it would run the terrible risk of hearing grotesque, suggestive echoes of its own forgotten darkness, and falling victim to an avenging recrudescence of the mindless frenzy of the first beginnings.

I am not going to waste your time with examples of Conrad's famed evocation of the African atmosphere in *Heart of Darkness*. In the final consideration it amounts to no more than a steady, ponderous, fake-ritualistic repetition of two sentences, one about silence and the other about frenzy.

The eagle-eyed English critic F. R. Leavis drew attention nearly thirty years ago to Conrad's "adjectival insistence upon inexpressible and incomprehensible mystery." That insistence must not be dismissed lightly, as many Conrad critics have tended to do, as a mere stylistic flaw. For it raises serious questions of artistic good faith. When a writer while pretending to record scenes, incidents, and their impact is in reality engaged in inducing hypnotic stupor in his readers through a bombardment of emotive words and other forms of trickery, much more has to be at stake than stylistic felicity. Generally, normal readers are well armed to detect and resist such underhand activity. But Conrad chose his subject well—one which was guaranteed not to put him in conflict with the psychological predisposition of his readers or raise the need for him to contend with their resistance. He chose the role of purveyor of comforting myths.

The most interesting and revealing passages in *Heart of Darkness* are, however, about people. . . . Herein lies the meaning of *Heart of Darkness* and the fascination it holds over the Western mind: "What thrilled you was just the thought of their humanity—like yours . . . Ugly."

Having shown us Africa in the mass, Conrad then zeroes in, as you would say, half a page later, on a specific example, giving us one of his rare descriptions of an African who is not just limbs or rolling eyes:

> And between whiles I had to look after the savage who was fireman. He was an improved specimen; he could fire up a vertical boiler. He was there below me, and, upon my word, to look at him was as edifying as seeing a dog in a parody of breeches and a feather hat, walking on his hind legs. A few months of training had done for that really fine chap. He squinted at the steam gauge and at the water gauge with an evident effort of intrepidity—and he had filed his teeth, too, the poor devil, and the wool of his pate shaved into queer patterns, and three ornamental scars on each of his cheeks. . . .

As everybody knows, Conrad is a romantic on the side. He might not exactly admire savages clapping their hands and stamping their feet, but they have at least the merit of being in their place, unlike this dog in a parody of breeches. For Conrad, things being in their place is of the utmost importance.

"Fine fellows—cannibals—in their place," he tell us pointedly. Tragedy begins when things leave their accustomed place, like Europe leaving its safe stronghold between the policeman and the baker to take a peep into the heart of darkness. . . .

Towards the end of the story, Conrad lavishes a whole page quite unexpectedly on an African woman who has obviously been some kind of mistress to Mr. Kurtz and now presides (if I may be permitted a little imitation of Conrad) like a formidable mystery over the inexorable imminence of his departure. . . .

This Amazon is drawn in considerable detail, albeit of a predictable nature, for two reasons. First, she is in her place and so can win Conrad's special brand of approval, and, second, she fulfills a structural requirement of the story: a savage counterpart to the refined, European woman with whom the story will end. . . .

The difference in the attitude of the novelist to these two women is conveyed in too many direct and subtle ways to need elaboration. But perhaps the most significant difference is the one implied in the author's bestowal of human expression to the one and the withholding of it from the other. It is clearly not part of Conrad's purpose to confer language on the "rudimentary souls" of Africa. They only "exchanged short grunting phrases" even among themselves, but mostly they were too busy with their frenzy. There are two occasions in the book, however, when Conrad departs somewhat from his practice and confers speech, even English speech, on the savages. The first occurs when cannibalism gets the better of them:

> "Catch 'im," he snapped, with a bloodshot widening of his eyes and a flash of sharp white teeth—"catch 'im. Give 'im to us." "To you, eh?" I asked; "what would you do with them?"
> "Eat 'im!" he said curtly.

The other occasion was the famous announcement:

> Mistah Kurtz—he dead. . . .

At first sight these instances might be mistaken for unexpected acts of generosity from Conrad. In reality they constitute some of his best assaults. In the case of the cannibals the incomprehensible grunts that had thus far served them for speech suddenly proved inadequate for Conrad's purpose of letting the European glimpse the unspeakable craving in their hearts. Weighing the necessity for consistency in the portrayal of the dumb brutes against the sensational advantages of securing their conviction by clear, unambiguous evidence issuing out of their own mouth, Conrad chose the latter. As for the announcement of Mr. Kurtz's death by the "insolent black head in the doorway," what better or more appropriate *finis* could be written to the horror story of that wayward child of civilization who wilfully had given his soul to the powers of darkness and "taken a high seat amongst the devils of the land" than the proclamation of his physical death by the forces he had joined?

It might be contended, of course, that the attitude to the African in *Heart of Darkness* is not Conrad's but that of his fictional narrator,

Marlow, and that far from endorsing it Conrad might indeed be holding it up to irony and criticism. Certainly Conrad appears to go to considerable pains to set up layers of insulation between himself and the moral universe of his story. He has, for example, a narrator behind a narrator. . . . But if Conrad's intention is to draw a *cordon sanitaire* between himself and the moral and psychological malaise of his narrator, his care seems to me totally wasted because he neglects to hint however subtly or tentatively at an alternative frame of reference by which we may judge the actions and opinions of his characters. It would not have been beyond Conrad's power to make that provision if he had thought it necessary. Marlow seems to me to enjoy Conrad's complete confidence—a feeling reinforced by the close similarities between their two careers. . . .

The kind of liberalism espoused here by Marlow/Conrad touched all the best minds of the age in England, Europe, and America. It took different forms in the minds of different people but almost always managed to sidestep the ultimate question of equality between white people and black people. . . .

[Conrad] would not use the word brother however qualified; the farthest he would go was kinship. . . .

It is important to note that Conrad, careful as ever with his words, is not talking so much about *distant kinship* as about someone *laying a claim* on it. The black man lays a claim on the white man which is well-nigh intolerable. It is the laying of this claim which frightens and at the same time fascinates Conrad, "the thought of their humanity—like yours . . . Ugly."

The point of my observations should be quite clear by now, namely that Conrad was a bloody racist. That this simple truth is glossed over in criticisms of his work is due to the fact that white racism against Africa is such a normal way of thinking that its manifestations go completely undetected. Students of *Heart of Darkness* will often tell you that Conrad is concerned not so much with Africa as with the deterioration of one European mind caused by solitude and sickness. They will point out to you that Conrad is, if anything, less charitable to the Europeans in the story than he is to the natives. A Conrad student told me in Scotland last year that

Africa is merely a setting for the disintegration of the mind of Mr. Kurtz.

Which is partly the point. Africa as setting and backdrop which eliminates the African as human factor. Africa as a metaphysical battlefield devoid of all recognizable humanity, into which the wandering European enters at his peril. Of course, there is a preposterous and perverse kind of arrogance in thus reducing Africa to the role of props for the breakup of one petty European mind. But that is not even the point. The real question is the dehumanization of Africa and Africans which this age-long attitude has fostered and continues to foster in the world. And the question is whether a novel which celebrates this dehumanization, which depersonalizes a portion of the human race, can be called a great work of art. My answer is: No, it cannot. I would not call that man an artist, for example, who composes an eloquent instigation to one people to fall upon another and destroy them. No matter how striking his imagery or how beautiful his cadences fall, such a man is no more a great artist than another may be called a priest who reads the mass backwards or a physician who poisons his patients. . . .

Naturally, Conrad is a dream for psychoanalytic critics. Perhaps the most detailed study of him in this direction is by Bernard C. Meyer, M.D. In his lengthy book, Dr. Meyer follows every conceivable lead (and sometimes inconceivable ones) to explain Conrad. As an example, he gives us long disquisitions on the significance of hair and haircutting in Conrad. And yet not even one word is spared for his attitude to black people. Not even the discussion of Conrad's anti-semitism was enough to spark off in Dr. Meyer's mind those other dark and explosive thoughts. Which only leads one to surmise that Western psychoanalysts must regard the kind of racism displayed by Conrad as absolutely normal despite the profoundly important work done by Frantz Fanon in the psychiatric hospitals in French Algeria. . . .

There are two probable grounds on which what I have said so far may be contested. The first is that it is no concern of fiction to please people about whom it is written. I will go along with that. But

I am not talking about pleasing people. I am talking about a book which parades in the most vulgar fashion prejudices and insults from which a section of mankind has suffered untold agonies and atrocities in the past and continues to do so in many ways and many places today. I am talking about a story in which the very humanity of black people is called in question. It seems to me totally inconceivable that great art or even good art could possibly reside in such unwholesome surroundings.

Secondly, I may be challenged on the grounds of actuality. Conrad, after all, sailed down the Congo in 1890 when my own father was still a babe in arms, and recorded what he saw. How could I stand up in 1975, fifty years after his death, and purport to contradict him? My answer is that as a sensible man I will not accept just any traveller's tales solely on the grounds that I have not made the journey myself. I will not trust the evidence even of a man's very eyes when I suspect them to be as jaundiced as Conrad's. And we also happen to know that Conrad was, in the words of his biographer, Bernard C. Meyer, "notoriously inaccurate in the rendering of his own history."

But more important by far is the abundant testimony about Conrad's savages which we could gather if we were so inclined from other sources and which might lead us to think that these people must have had other occupations besides merging into the evil forest or materializing out of it simply to plague Marlow and his dispirited band. . . .

Conrad did not originate the image of Africa which we find in his book. It was and is the dominant image of Africa in the Western imagination, and Conrad merely brought the peculiar gifts of his own mind to bear on it. . . . Africa is to Europe as the picture is to Dorian Gray—a carrier onto whom the master unloads his physical and moral deformities so that he may go forward, erect and immaculate. Consequently, Africa is something to be avoided, just as the picture has to be hidden away to safeguard the man's jeopardous integrity. Keep away from Africa, or else! Mr. Kurtz of *Heart of Darkness* should have heeded that warning, and the prowling horror in his heart would have kept its place, chained to its lair. But he foolishly exposed himself to the wild irresistible allure of the jungle, and lo! the darkness found him out. . . .

Ultimately, the abandonment of unwholesome thoughts must be its own and only reward. Although I have used the word *wilful* a few times in this talk to characterize the West's view of Africa, it may well be that what is happening at this stage is more akin to reflex action than calculated malice. Which does not make the situation more but less hopeful. . . .

[Although] the work which needs to be done may appear too daunting, I believe that it is not one day too soon to begin.

From "An Image of Africa," *The Massachusetts Review,* 1977

PHILIP GOUREVITCH

In Rwanda in 1994 the government had adopted a new policy, according to which everyone in the country's Hutu majority group was called upon to murder everyone in the Tutsi minority. The government, and an astounding number of its subjects, imagined that by exterminating the Tutsi people they could make the world a better place, and the mass killing had followed.

All at once, as it seemed, something we could have only imagined was upon us—and we could still only imagine it. This is what fascinates me most in existence: the peculiar necessity of imagining what is, in fact, real. During the months of killing in 1994, as I followed the news from Rwanda, and later, when I read that the United Nations had decided, for the first time in its history, that it needed to use the word "genocide" to describe what had happened, I was repeatedly reminded of the moment, near the end of Conrad's *Heart of Darkness*, when the narrator Marlow is back in Europe, and his aunt, finding him depleted, fusses over his health. "It was not my strength that wanted nursing," Marlow says, "it was my imagination that wanted soothing."

I took Marlow's condition on returning from Africa as my point of departure. I wanted to know how Rwandans understood what had happened in their country, and how they were getting on in the aftermath. The word "genocide" and the images of the nameless and numberless dead left too much to the imagination.

From *We Wish to Inform You That Tomorrow We Will Be Killed with Our Families*, 1998

HEART OF
DARKNESS

I

The *Nellie*, a cruising yawl, swung to her anchor without a flutter of the sails, and was at rest. The flood had made, the wind was nearly calm, and being bound down the river, the only thing for it was to come to and wait for the turn of the tide.

The sea-reach of the Thames stretched before us like the beginning of an interminable waterway. In the offing the sea and the sky were welded together without a joint, and in the luminous space the tanned sails of the barges drifting up with the tide seemed to stand still in red clusters of canvas sharply peaked, with gleams of varnished sprits. A haze rested on the low shores that ran out to sea in vanishing flatness. The air was dark above Gravesend, and farther back still seemed condensed into a mournful gloom, brooding motionless over the biggest, and the greatest, town on earth.

The Director of Companies was our captain and our host. We four affectionately watched his back as he stood in the bows looking to seaward. On the whole river there was nothing that looked half so nautical. He resembled a pilot, which to a seaman is trustworthiness personified. It was difficult to realize his work was not out there in the luminous estuary, but behind him, within the brooding gloom.

Between us there was, as I have already said somewhere, the bond of the sea. Besides holding our hearts together through long periods of separation, it had the effect of making us tolerant of each other's yarns—and even convictions. The Lawyer—the best of old fellows—had, because of his many years and many virtues, the only cushion on deck, and was lying on the only rug. The Accountant had brought out already a box of dominoes, and was toying architecturally with the bones. Marlow sat cross-legged right aft, leaning against the mizzen-mast. He had sunken cheeks, a yellow complexion, a straight back, an ascetic aspect, and, with his arms dropped, the palms of hands outwards, resembled an idol. The Director, satisfied the anchor had good hold, made his way aft and sat down amongst us. We exchanged a few words lazily. Afterwards there was silence on board the yacht. For some reason or other we did not begin that game of dominoes. We felt meditative, and fit for nothing but placid staring. The day was ending in a serenity of still and exquisite brilliance. The water shone pacifically; the sky, without a speck, was a benign immensity of unstained light; the very mist on the Essex marshes was like a gauzy and radiant fabric, hung from the wooded rises inland, and draping the low shores in diaphanous folds. Only the gloom to the west, brooding over the upper reaches, became more sombre every minute, as if angered by the approach of the sun.

And at last, in its curved and imperceptible fall, the sun sank low, and from glowing white changed to a dull red without rays and without heat, as if about to go out suddenly, stricken to death by the touch of that gloom brooding over a crowd of men.

Forthwith a change came over the waters, and the serenity became less brilliant but more profound. The old river in its broad reach rested unruffled at the decline of day, after ages of good service done to the race that peopled its banks, spread out in the tranquil dignity of a waterway leading to the uttermost ends of the earth. We looked at the venerable stream not in the vivid flush of a short day that comes and departs for ever, but in the august light of abiding memories. And indeed nothing is easier for a man who has, as the phrase goes, "followed the sea" with reverence and affection, than to evoke the great spirit of the past upon the lower reaches of the Thames. The tidal current runs to and fro in its unceasing service, crowded with memories of men and ships it had borne to the rest of home or to the battles of the sea. It had known and served all the men of whom the nation is proud, from Sir Francis Drake to Sir John Franklin, knights all, titled and untitled—the great knights-errant of the sea. It had borne all the ships whose names are like jewels flashing in the night of time, from the *Golden Hind* returning with her round flanks full of treasure, to be visited by the Queen's Highness and thus pass out of the gigantic tale, to the *Erebus* and *Terror,* bound on other conquests—and that never returned. It had known the ships and the men. They had sailed from Deptford, from Greenwich, from Erith—the adventurers and the settlers; kings' ships and the ships of men on 'Change; captains, admirals, the dark "interlopers" of the Eastern trade, and the commissioned "generals" of East India fleets. Hunters for gold or pursuers of fame, they all had gone out on that stream, bearing the sword, and often the torch, messengers of the might within the land, bearers of a spark from the sacred fire. What greatness had not floated on the ebb of that river into the mystery of an unknown earth! . . . The dreams of men, the seed of commonwealths, the germs of empires.

The sun set; the dusk fell on the stream, and lights began to appear along the shore. The Chapman lighthouse, a three-legged thing erect on a mud-flat, shone strongly. Lights of ships moved in the fairway—a great stir of lights going up and going down. And farther west on the upper reaches the place of the monstrous town was still marked ominously on the sky, a brooding gloom in sunshine, a lurid glare under the stars.

"And this also," said Marlow suddenly, "has been one of the dark places of the earth." — dark -

He was the only man of us who still "followed the sea." The worst that could be said of him was that he did not represent his class. He was a seaman, but he was a wanderer, too, while most seamen lead, if one may so express it, a sedentary life. Their minds are of the stay-at-home order, and their home is always with them—the ship; and so is their country—the sea. One ship is very much

like another, and the sea is always the same. In the immutability of
their surroundings the foreign shores, the foreign faces, the chang-
ing immensity of life, glide past, veiled not by a sense of mystery
but by a slightly disdainful ignorance; for there is nothing mysterious to a seaman unless it be the sea itself, which is the mistress of
his existence and as inscrutable as Destiny. For the rest, after his
hours of work, a casual stroll or a casual spree on shore suffices to
unfold for him the secret of a whole continent, and generally he
finds the secret not worth knowing. The yarns of seamen have a direct simplicity, the whole meaning of which lies within the shell of
a cracked nut. But Marlow was not typical (if his propensity to spin
yarns be excepted), and to him the meaning of an episode was not
inside like a kernel but outside, enveloping the tale which brought
it out only as a glow brings out a haze, in the likeness of one of these
misty halos that sometimes are made visible by the spectral illumination of moonshine.

His remark did not seem at all surprising. It was just like Marlow.
It was accepted in silence. No one took the trouble to grunt even;
and presently he said, very slow—

"I was thinking of very old times, when the Romans first came
here, nineteen hundred years ago—the other day . . . Light came out
of this river since—you say Knights? Yes; but it is like a running
blaze on a plain, like a flash of lightning in the clouds. We live in the
flicker—may it last as long as the old earth keeps rolling! But darkness was here yesterday. Imagine the feelings of a commander of a
fine—what d'ye call 'em?—trireme in the Mediterranean, ordered
suddenly to the north; run overland across the Gauls in a hurry; put
in charge of one of these craft the legionaries—a wonderful lot of
handy men they must have been, too—used to build, apparently by
the hundred, in a month or two, if we may believe what we read.
Imagine him here—the very end of the world, a sea the colour of
lead, a sky the colour of smoke, a kind of ship about as rigid as a
concertina—and going up this river with stores, or orders, or what
you like. Sand-banks, marshes, forests, savages,—precious little to
eat fit for a civilized man, nothing but Thames water to drink. No
Falernian wine here, no going ashore. Here and there a military

camp lost in a wilderness, like a needle in a bundle of hay—cold, fog, tempests, disease, exile, and death—death skulking in the air, in the water, in the bush. They must have been dying like flies here. Oh, yes—he did it. Did it very well, too, no doubt, and without thinking much about it either, except afterwards to brag of what he had done through his time, perhaps. They were men enough to face the darkness. And perhaps he was cheered by keeping his eye on a chance of promotion to the fleet at Ravenna by-and-by, if he had good friends in Rome and survived the awful climate. Or think of a decent young citizen in a toga—perhaps too much dice, you know—coming out here in the train of some prefect, or tax-gatherer, or trader even, to mend his fortunes. Land in a swamp, march through the woods, and in some inland post feel the savagery, the utter savagery, had closed round him,—all that mysterious life of the wilderness that stirs in the forest, in the jungles, in the hearts of wild men. There's no initiation either into such mysteries. He has to live in the midst of the incomprehensible, which is also detestable. And it has a fascination, too, that goes to work upon him. The fascination of the abomination—you know, imagine the growing regrets, the longing to escape, the powerless disgust, the surrender, the hate."

He paused.

"Mind," he began again, lifting one arm from the elbow, the palm of the hand outwards, so that, with his legs folded before him, he had the pose of a Buddha preaching in European clothes and without a lotus-flower— "Mind, none of us would feel exactly like this. What saves us is efficiency—the devotion to efficiency. But these chaps were not much account, really. They were no colonists; their administration was merely a squeeze, and nothing more, I suspect. They were conquerors, and for that you want only brute force— nothing to boast of, when you have it, since your strength is just an accident arising from the weakness of others. They grabbed what they could get for the sake of what was to be got. It was just robbery with violence, aggravated murder on a great scale, and men going at it blind—as is very proper for those who tackle a darkness. The conquest of the earth, which mostly means the taking it away from those who have a different complexion or slightly flatter noses than ourselves, is not a pretty thing when you look into it too much. What redeems it is the idea only. An idea at the back of it; not a sentimental pretence but an idea; and an unselfish belief in the idea—something you can set up, and bow down before, and offer a sacrifice to . . ."

He broke off. Flames glided in the river, small green flames, red flames, white flames, pursuing, overtaking, joining, crossing each other—then separating slowly or hastily. The traffic of the great city went on in the deepening night upon the sleepless river. We looked on, waiting patiently—there was nothing else to do till the end of the flood; but it was only after a long silence, when he said, in a hesitating voice, "I suppose you fellows remember I did once turn fresh-water sailor for a bit," that we knew we were fated, before the ebb began to run, to hear about one of Marlow's inconclusive experiences.

"I don't want to bother you much with what happened to me personally," he began, showing in this remark the weakness of many tellers of tales who seem so often unaware of what their audience would best like to hear; "yet to understand the effect of it on me you ought to know how I got out there, what I saw, how I went up that river to the place where I first met the poor chap. It was the farthest point of navigation and the culminating point of my experience. It seemed somehow to throw a kind of light on everything about me—and into my thoughts. It was sombre enough, too—and pitiful—not extraordinary in any way—not very clear either. No, not very clear. And yet it seemed to throw a kind of light.

"I had then, as you remember, just returned to London after a lot of Indian Ocean, Pacific, China Seas—a regular dose of the East—six years or so, and I was loafing about, hindering you fellows in your work and invading your homes, just as though I had got a heavenly mission to civilize you. It was very fine for a time, but after a bit I did get tired of resting. Then I began to look for a ship—I should think the hardest work on earth. But the ships wouldn't even look at me. And I got tired of that game, too.

"Now when I was a little chap I had a passion for maps. I would look for hours at South America, or Africa, or Australia, and lose

light 'n dark~Marlow has
A darkness

myself in all the glories of exploration. At that time there were many blank spaces on the earth, and when I saw one that looked particularly inviting on a map (but they all look that) I would put my finger on it and say, When I grow up I will go there. The North Pole was one of these places, I remember. Well, I haven't been there yet, and shall not try now. The glamour's off. Other places were scattered about the Equator, and in every sort of latitude all over the two hemispheres. I have been in some of them, and ... well, we won't talk about that. But there was one yet—the biggest, the most blank, so to speak—that I had a hankering after.

"True, by this time it was not a blank space any more. It had got filled since my boyhood with rivers and lakes and names. It had ceased to be a blank space of delightful mystery—a white patch for a boy to dream gloriously over. It had become a place of darkness. But there was in it one river especially, a mighty big river, that you could see on the map, resembling an immense snake uncoiled, with its head in the sea, its body at rest curving afar over a vast country, and its tail lost in the depths of the land. And as I looked at the map of it in a shop-window, it fascinated me as a snake would a bird—a silly little bird. Then I remembered there was a big concern, a Company for trade on that river. Dash it all! I thought to myself, they can't trade without using some kind of craft on that lot of fresh water—steamboats! Why shouldn't I try to get charge of one? I went on along Fleet Street, but could not shake off the idea. The snake had charmed me.

"You understand it was a Continental concern, that Trading society; but I have a lot of relations living on the Continent, because it's cheap and not so nasty as it looks, they say.

"I am sorry to own I began to worry them. This was already a fresh departure for me. I was not used to get things that way, you know. I always went my own road and on my own legs where I had a mind to go. I wouldn't have believed it of myself; but, then—you see—I felt somehow I must get there by hook or by crook. So I worried them. The men said 'My dear fellow,' and did nothing. Then— would you believe it?—I tried the women. I, Charlie Marlow, set the women to work—to get a job. Heavens! Well, you see, the notion drove me. I had an aunt, a dear enthusiastic soul. She wrote: 'It will be delightful. I am ready to do anything, anything for you. It is a glorious idea. I know the wife of a very high personage in the Administration, and also a man who has lots of influence with,' etc., etc. She was determined to make no end of fuss to get me appointed skipper of a river steamboat, if such was my fancy.

"I got my appointment—of course; and I got it very quick. It appears the Company had received news that one of their captains had been killed in a scuffle with the natives. This was my chance, and it made me the more anxious to go. It was only months and months afterwards, when I made the attempt to recover what was left of the body, that I heard the original quarrel arose from a misunderstanding about some hens. Yes, two black hens. Fresleven—that was the fellow's name, a Dane—thought himself wronged somehow in the bargain, so he went ashore and started to hammer the chief of the village with a stick. Oh, it didn't surprise me in the least to hear this, and at the same time to be told that Fresleven was the gentlest, quietest creature that ever walked on two legs. No doubt he was; but he had been a couple of years already out there engaged in the noble cause, you know, and he probably felt the need at last of asserting his self-respect in some way. Therefore he whacked the old nigger mercilessly, while a big crowd of his people watched him, thunderstruck, till some man—I was told the chief's son—in desperation at hearing the old chap yell, made a tentative jab with a spear at the white man—and of course it went quite easy between the shoulder-blades. Then the whole population cleared into the forest, expecting all kinds of calamities to happen, while, on the other hand, the steamer Fresleven commanded left also in a bad panic, in charge of the engineer, I believe. Afterwards nobody seemed to trouble much about Fresleven's remains, till I got out and stepped into his shoes. I couldn't let it rest, though; but when an opportunity offered at last to meet my predecessor, the grass growing through his ribs was tall enough to hide his bones. They were all there. The supernatural being had not been touched after he fell. And the village was deserted, the huts gaped black, rotting, all askew within the fallen enclosures. A calamity had come to it, sure enough. The people had vanished. Mad terror had scattered them, men, women, and children, through the bush, and they had never returned. What became of the hens I don't know either. I should think the cause of progress got them, anyhow. However, through this glorious affair I got my appointment, before I had fairly begun to hope for it.

"I flew around like mad to get ready, and before forty-eight hours I was crossing the Channel to show myself to my employers, and sign the contract. In a very few hours I arrived in a city that always makes me think of a whited sepulchre. Prejudice no doubt. I had no difficulty in finding the Company's offices. It was the biggest thing in the town, and everybody I met was full of it. They were going to run an over-sea empire, and make no end of coin by trade.

"A narrow and deserted street in deep shadow, high houses, innumerable windows with venetian blinds, a dead silence, grass sprouting between the stones, imposing carriage archways right and left, immense double doors standing ponderously ajar. I slipped through one of these cracks, went up a swept and ungarnished staircase, as arid as a desert, and opened the first door I came to. Two women, one fat and the other slim, sat on straw-bottomed chairs, knitting black wool. The slim one got up and walked straight at me—still knitting with downcast eyes—and only just as I began to think of getting out of her way, as you would for a somnambulist, stood still, and looked up. Her dress was as plain as an umbrella-cover, and she turned round without a word and preceded me into a waiting-room. I gave my name, and looked about. Deal table in the middle, plain chairs all round the walls, on one end a large shining map, marked with all the colours of a rainbow. There was a vast amount of red—good to see at any time, because one knows that some real work is done in there, a deuce of a lot of blue, a little green, smears of orange, and, on the East Coast, a purple patch, to show where the jolly pioneers of progress drink the jolly lager-beer. However, I wasn't going into any of these. I was going into the yellow. Dead in the centre. And the river was there—fascinating—deadly—like a snake. Ough! A door opened, a white-haired secretarial head, but wearing a compassionate expression, appeared, and a skinny forefinger beckoned me into the sanctuary. Its light was dim, and a heavy writing-desk squatted in the middle. From behind that structure came out an impression of pale plumpness in a frock-coat. The great man himself. He was five feet six, I should judge, and had his grip on the handle-end of ever so many millions. He shook hands, I fancy, murmured vaguely, was satisfied with my French. *Bon voyage.*

"In about forty-five seconds I found myself again in the waiting-room with the compassionate secretary, who, full of desolation and sympathy, made me sign some document. I believe I undertook amongst other things not to disclose any trade secrets. Well, I am not going to.

"I began to feel slightly uneasy. You know I am not used to such ceremonies, and there was something ominous in the atmosphere. It was just as though I had been let into some conspiracy—I don't know—something not quite right; and I was glad to get out. In the outer room the two women knitted black wool feverishly. People were arriving, and the younger one was walking back and forth introducing them. The old one sat on her chair. Her flat cloth slippers were propped up on a foot-warmer, and a cat reposed on her lap. She wore a starched white affair on her head, had a wart on one cheek, and silver-rimmed spectacles hung on the tip of her nose. She glanced at me above the glasses. The swift and indifferent placidity of that look troubled me. Two youths with foolish and cheery countenances were being piloted over, and she threw at them the same quick glance of unconcerned wisdom. She seemed to know all about them and about me, too. An eerie feeling came over me. She seemed uncanny and fateful. Often far away there I thought of these two, guarding the door of Darkness, knitting black wool as for a warm pall, one introducing, introducing continuously to the unknown, the other scrutinizing the cheery and foolish faces with unconcerned old eyes. *Ave!* Old knitter of black wool. *Morituri te salutant.* Not many of those she looked at ever saw her again—not half, by a long way.

"There was yet a visit to the doctor. 'A simple formality,' assured me the secretary, with an air of taking an immense part in all my sorrows. Accordingly a young chap wearing his hat over the left eyebrow, some clerk I suppose—there must have been clerks in the business, though the house was as still as a house in a city of the dead—came from somewhere upstairs, and led me forth. He was shabby and careless, with ink-stains on the sleeves of his jacket, and his cravat was large and billowy, under a chin shaped like the toe of an old boot. It was a little too early for the doctor, so I proposed a drink, and thereupon he developed a vein of joviality. As we sat over our vermouths he glorified the Company's business, and by-and-by I expressed casually my surprise at him not going out there. He became very cool and collected all at once. 'I am not such a fool as I look, quoth Plato to his disciples,' he said sententiously, emptied his glass with great resolution, and we rose.

"The old doctor felt my pulse, evidently thinking of something else the while. 'Good, good for there,' he mumbled, and then with a certain eagerness asked me whether I would let him measure my head. Rather surprised, I said Yes, when he produced a thing like calipers and got the dimensions back and front and every way taking notes carefully. He was an unshaven little man in a threadbare coat like a gaberdine, with his feet in slippers, and I thought him a harmless fool. 'I always ask leave, in the interests of science, to measure the crania of those going out there,' he said. 'And when they come back, too?' I asked. 'Oh, I never see them,' he remarked; 'and, moreover, the changes take place inside, you know.' He smiled, as if at some quiet joke. 'So you are going out there. Famous. Interesting, too.' He gave me a searching glance, and made another note. 'Ever any madness in your family?' he asked, in a matter-of-fact tone. I felt very annoyed. 'Is that question in the interests of science, too?' 'It would be,' he said, without taking notice of my irritation, 'interesting for science to watch the mental changes of individuals, on the spot, but . . .' 'Are you an <u>alienist</u>?' I interrupted. 'Every doctor should be—a little,' answered that original, imperturbably. 'I have a little theory which you Messieurs who go out there must help me to prove. This is my share in the advantages my country shall reap from the possession of such a magnificent dependency. The mere wealth I leave to others. Pardon my questions, but you are the first

Englishman coming under my observation . . .' I hastened to assure him I was not in the least typical. 'If I were,' said I, 'I wouldn't be talking like this with you.' 'What you say is rather profound, and probably erroneous,' he said, with a laugh. 'Avoid irritation more than exposure to the sun. Adieu. How do you English say, eh? Good-bye. Ah! Good-bye. Adieu. In the tropics one must before everything keep calm.' . . . He lifted a warning forefinger . . . '*Du calme, du calme. Adieu.*'

"One thing more remained to do—say good-bye to my excellent aunt. I found her triumphant. I had a cup of tea—the last decent cup of tea for many days—and in a room that most soothingly looked just as you would expect a lady's drawing-room to look, we had a long quiet chat by the fireside. In the course of these confidences it became quite plain to me I had been represented to the wife of the high dignitary, and goodness knows to how many more people besides, as an exceptional and gifted creature—a piece of good fortune for the Company—a man you don't get hold of every day. Good heavens! and I was going to take charge of a two-penny-half-penny river steamboat with a penny whistle attached! It appeared, however, I was also one of the Workers, with a capital—you know. Something like an emissary of light, something like a lower sort of apostle. There had been a lot of such rot let loose in print and talk just about that time, and the excellent woman, living right in the rush of all that humbug, got carried off her feet. She talked about 'weaning those ignorant millions from their horrid ways,' till, upon my word, she made me quite uncomfortable. I ventured to hint that the Company was run for profit.

" 'You forget, dear Charlie, that the labourer is worthy of his hire,' she said, brightly. It's queer how out of touch with truth women are. They live in a world of their own, and there has never been anything like it, and never can be. It is too beautiful altogether, and if they were to set it up it would go to pieces before the first sunset. Some confounded fact we men have been living contentedly with ever since the day of creation would start up and knock the whole thing over.

"After this I got embraced, told to wear flannel, be sure to write often, and so on—and I left. In the street—I don't know why—a queer feeling came to me that I was an impostor. Odd thing that I, who used to clear out for any part of the world at twenty-four hours' notice, with less thought than most men give to the crossing of a street, had a moment—I won't say of hesitation, but of startled pause, before this commonplace affair. The best way I can explain it to you is by saying that, for a second or two, I felt as though, instead of going to the centre of a continent, I were about to set off for the centre of the earth.

"I left in a French steamer, and she called in every blamed port they have out there, for, as far as I could see, the sole purpose of landing soldiers and custom-house officers. I watched the coast. Watching a coast as it slips by the ship is like thinking about an enigma. There it is before you—smiling, frowning, inviting, grand, mean, insipid, or savage, and always mute with an air of whispering, Come and find out. This one was almost featureless, as if still in the making, with an aspect of monotonous grimness. The edge of a colossal jungle, so dark-green as to be almost black, fringed with white surf, ran straight, like a ruled line, far, far away along a blue sea whose glitter was blurred by a creeping mist. The sun was fierce, the land seemed to glisten and drip with steam. Here and there greyish-whitish specks showed up clustered inside the white surf, with a flag flying above them perhaps. Settlements some centuries old, and still no bigger than pinheads on the untouched expanse of their background. We pounded along, stopped, landed soldiers; went on, landed custom-house clerks to levy toll in what looked like a God-forsaken wilderness, with a tin shed and a flag-pole lost in it; landed more soldiers—to take care of the custom-house clerks, presumably. Some, I heard, got drowned in the surf; but whether they did or not, nobody seemed particularly to care. They were just flung out there, and on we went. Every day the coast looked the same, as though we had not moved; but we passed various places—trading places—with names like Gran' Bassam, Little Popo; names that seemed to belong to some sordid farce acted in front of a sinister back-cloth. The idleness of a passenger, my isolation amongst all these men with whom I had no point of contact, the oily and languid sea, the uniform sombreness of the coast, seemed to keep me away from the truth of things, within the toil of a mournful and senseless delusion. The voice of the surf now and then was a positive pleasure, like the speech of a brother. It was something natural, that had its reason, that had a meaning. Now and then a boat from the shore gave one a momentary contact with reality. It was paddled by black fellows. You could see from afar the white of their eyeballs glistening. They shouted, sang; their bodies streamed with perspiration; they had faces like grotesque masks—these chaps; but they had bone, muscle, a wild vitality, an intense energy of movement, that was as natural and true as the surf along their coast. They wanted no excuse for being there. They were a great comfort to look at. For a time I would feel I belonged still to a world of straightforward facts; but the feeling would not last long. Something would turn up to scare it away. Once, I remember, we came upon a man-of-war anchored off the coast. There wasn't even a shed there, and she was shelling the bush. It appears the French had one of their wars going on thereabouts. Her ensign drooped limp like a rag; the muzzles of the long six-inch guns stuck out all over the low hull; the greasy, slimy swell swung her up lazily and let her down, swaying her thin masts. In the empty immensity of earth, sky, and water, there she was, incomprehensible, firing into a continent. Pop, would go one of the six-inch guns; a small flame would dart and vanish, a little white smoke would disappear, a tiny projectile would give a feeble screech—and nothing happened. Nothing could happen. There was a touch of insanity in the proceeding, a sense of lugubrious drollery in the sight; and it was not dissipated by somebody on board assuring me earnestly there was a camp of natives—he called them enemies!—hidden out of sight somewhere.

"We gave her her letters (I heard the men in that lonely ship were dying of fever at the rate of three a-day) and went on. We called at some more places with farcical names, where the merry dance of death and trade goes on in a still and earthy atmosphere as of an overheated catacomb; all along the formless coast bordered by dangerous surf, as if Nature herself had tried to ward off intruders; in and out of rivers, streams of death in life, whose banks were rotting into mud, whose waters, thickened into slime, invaded the contorted mangroves, that seemed to writhe at us in the extremity of an impotent despair. Nowhere did we stop long enough to get a particularized impression, but the general sense of vague and oppressive wonder grew upon me. It was like a weary pilgrimage amongst hints for nightmares.

"It was upward of thirty days before I saw the mouth of the big river. We anchored off the seat of the government. But my work would not begin till some two hundred miles farther on. So as soon as I could I made a start for a place thirty miles higher up.

"I had my passage on a little sea-going steamer. Her captain was a Swede, and knowing me for a seaman, invited me on the bridge. He was a young man, lean, fair, and morose, with lanky hair and a shuffling gait. As we left the miserable little wharf, he tossed his head contemptuously at the shore. 'Been living there?' he asked. I said, 'Yes.' 'Fine lot these government chaps—are they not?' he went on, speaking English with great precision and considerable bitterness. 'It is funny what some people will do for a few francs a-month. I wonder what becomes of that kind when it goes up country?' I said to him I expected to see that soon. 'So-o-o!' he exclaimed. He shuffled athwart, keeping one eye ahead vigilantly. 'Don't be too sure,' he continued. 'The other day I took up a man who hanged himself on the road. He was a Swede, too.' 'Hanged himself! Why, in God's name?' I cried. He kept on looking out watchfully. 'Who knows? The sun too much for him, or the country perhaps.'

"At last we opened a reach. A rocky cliff appeared, mounds of turned-up earth by the shore, houses on a hill, others with iron roofs, amongst a waste of excavations, or hanging to the declivity. A continuous noise of the rapids above hovered over this scene of inhabited devastation. A lot of people, mostly black and naked, moved about like ants. A jetty projected into the river. A blinding sunlight drowned all this at times in a sudden recrudescence of glare. 'There's your Company's station,' said the Swede, pointing to three wooden barrack-like structures on the rocky slope. 'I will send your things up. Four boxes did you say? So. Farewell.'

"I came upon a boiler wallowing in the grass, then found a path leading up the hill. It turned aside for the boulders, and also for an undersized railway-truck lying there on its back with its wheels in the air. One was off. The thing looked as dead as the carcass of some animal. I came upon more pieces of decaying machinery, a stack of rusty rails. To the left a clump of trees made a shady spot, where dark things seemed to stir feebly. I blinked, the path was steep. A horn tooted to the right, and I saw the black people run. A heavy and dull detonation shook the ground, a puff of smoke came out of the cliff, and that was all. No change appeared on the face of the rock. They were building a railway. The cliff was not in the way of anything; but this objectless blasting was all the work going on.

"A slight clinking behind me made me turn my head. Six black men advanced in a file, toiling up the path. They walked erect and slow, balancing small baskets full of earth on their heads, and the clink kept time with their footsteps. Black rags were wound round their loins, and the short ends behind waggled to and fro like tails. I could see every rib, the joints of their limbs were like knots in a rope; each had an iron collar on his neck, and all were connected together with a chain whose bights swung between them, rhythmically clinking. Another report from the cliff made me think suddenly of that ship of war I had seen firing into a continent. It was the same kind of ominous voice; but these men could by no stretch of imagination be called enemies. They were called criminals, and the outraged law, like the bursting shells, had come to them, an insoluble mystery from the sea. All their meagre breasts panted together, the violently dilated nostrils quivered, the eyes stared stonily uphill. They passed me within six inches, without a glance, with that complete, deathlike indifference of unhappy savages. Behind this raw matter one of the reclaimed, the product of the new forces at work, strolled despondently, carrying a rifle by its middle. He had a uniform jacket with one button off, and seeing a white man on the path, hoisted his weapon to his shoulder with alacrity. This was simple prudence, white men being so much alike at a distance that he could not tell who I might be. He was speedily reassured, and with a large, white, rascally grin, and a glance at his charge, seemed to take me into partnership in his exalted trust.

After all, I also was a part of the great cause of these high and just proceedings.

"Instead of going up, I turned and descended to the left. My idea was to let that chain-gang get out of sight before I climbed the hill. You know I am not particularly tender; I've had to strike and to fend off. I've had to resist and to attack sometimes—that's only one way of resisting—without counting the exact cost, according to the demands of such sort of life as I had blundered into. I've seen the devil of violence, and the devil of greed, and the devil of hot desire; but, by all the stars! these were strong, lusty, red-eyed devils, that swayed and drove men—men, I tell you. But as I stood on this hillside, I foresaw that in the blinding sunshine of that land I would become acquainted with a flabby, pretending, weak-eyed devil of a rapacious and pitiless folly. How insidious he could be, too, I was only to find out several months later and a thousand miles farther. For a moment I stood appalled, as though by a warning. Finally I descended the hill, obliquely, towards the trees I had seen.

"I avoided a vast artificial hole somebody had been digging on the slope, the purpose of which I found it impossible to divine. It wasn't a quarry or a sandpit, anyhow. It was just a hole. It might have been connected with the philanthropic desire of giving the criminals something to do. I don't know. Then I nearly fell into a very narrow ravine, almost no more than a scar in the hillside. I discovered that a lot of imported drainage-pipes for the settlement had been tumbled in there. There wasn't one that was not broken. It was a wanton smash-up. At last I got under the trees. My purpose was to stroll into the shade for a moment; but no sooner within than it seemed to me I had stepped into the gloomy circle of some Inferno. The rapids were near, and an uninterrupted, uniform, headlong, rushing noise filled the mournful stillness of the grove, where not a breath stirred, not a leaf moved, with a mysterious sound—as though the tearing pace of the launched earth had suddenly become audible.

"Black shapes crouched, lay, sat between the trees leaning against the trunks, clinging to the earth, half coming out, half effaced within the dim light, in all the attitudes of pain, abandonment, and despair. Another mine on the cliff went off, followed by a slight shudder of the soil under my feet. The work was going on. The work! And this was the place where some of the helpers had withdrawn to die.

"They were dying slowly—it was very clear. They were not enemies, they were not criminals, they were nothing earthly now,— nothing but black shadows of disease and starvation, lying confusedly in the greenish gloom. Brought from all the recesses of the coast in all the legality of time contracts, lost in uncongenial surroundings, fed on unfamiliar food, they sickened, became inefficient, and were then allowed to crawl away and rest. These moribund shapes were free as air—and nearly as thin. I began to distinguish the gleam of the eyes under the trees. Then, glancing down, I saw a face near my hand. The black bones reclined at full length with one shoulder against the tree, and slowly the eyelids rose and the sunken eyes looked up at me, enormous and vacant, a kind of blind, white flicker in the depths of the orbs, which died out slowly. The man seemed young—almost a boy—but you know with them it's hard to tell. I found nothing else to do but to offer him one of my good Swede's ship's biscuits I had in my pocket. The fingers closed slowly on it and held—there was no other movement and no other glance. He had tied a bit of white worsted round his neck— Why? Where did he get it? Was it a badge—an ornament—a charm—a propitiatory act? Was there any idea at all connected with it? It looked startling round his black neck, this bit of white thread from beyond the seas.

"Near the same tree two more bundles of acute angles sat with their legs drawn up. One, with his chin propped on his knees, stared at nothing, in an intolerable and appalling manner: his brother phantom rested its forehead, as if overcome with a great weariness; and all about others were scattered in every pose of contorted collapse, as in some picture of a massacre or a pestilence. While I stood horror-struck, one of these creatures rose to his hands and knees, and went off on all-fours towards the river to drink. He lapped out of his hand, then sat up in the sunlight, crossing his shins in front of him, and after a time let his woolly head fall on his breastbone.

"I didn't want any more loitering in the shade, and I made haste towards the station. When near the buildings I met a white man, in such an unexpected elegance of get-up that in the first moment I took him for a sort of vision. I saw a high starched collar, white cuffs, a light alpaca jacket, snowy trousers, a clean necktie, and varnished boots. No hat. Hair parted, brushed, oiled, under a green-lined parasol held in a big white hand. He was amazing, and had a penholder behind his ear.

"I shook hands with this miracle, and I learned he was the Company's chief accountant, and that all the bookkeeping was done at this station. He had come out for a moment, he said, 'to get a breath of fresh air.' The expression sounded wonderfully odd, with its suggestion of sedentary desk-life. I wouldn't have mentioned the fellow to you at all, only it was from his lips that I first heard the name of the man who is so indissolubly connected with the memories of that time. Moreover, I respected the fellow. Yes; I respected his collars, his vast cuffs, his brushed hair. His appearance was certainly that of a hairdresser's dummy; but in the great demoralization of the land he kept up his appearance. That's backbone. His starched collars and got-up shirt-fronts were achievements of character. He had been out nearly three years; and later, I could not help asking him how he managed to sport such linen. He had just the faintest blush, and said modestly, 'I've been teaching one of the native women about the station. It was difficult. She had a distaste for the work.' Thus this man had verily accomplished something. And he was devoted to his books, which were in apple-pie order.

"Everything else in the station was in a muddle—heads, things, buildings. Strings of dusty niggers with splay feet arrived and departed; a stream of manufactured goods, rubbishy cottons, beads, and brass wire sent into the depths of darkness, and in return came a precious trickle of ivory.

"I had to wait in the station for ten days—an eternity. I lived in a hut in the yard, but to be out of the chaos I would sometimes get into the accountant's office. It was built of horizontal planks, and so badly put together that, as he bent over his high desk, he was barred from neck to heels with narrow strips of sunlight. There was no need to open the big shutters to see. It was hot there, too; big flies buzzed fiendishly, and did not sting, but stabbed. I sat generally on the floor, while, of faultless appearance (and even slightly scented), perching on a high stool, he wrote. Sometimes he stood up for exercise. When a truckle-bed with a sick man (some invalid agent from up-country) was put in there, he exhibited a gentle annoyance. 'The groans of this sick person,' he said, 'distract my attention. And without that it is extremely difficult to guard against clerical errors in this climate.'

"One day he remarked, without lifting his head, 'In the interior you will no doubt meet Mr. Kurtz.' On my asking who Mr. Kurtz was, he said he was a first-class agent; and seeing my disappointment at this information, he added slowly, laying down his pen, 'He is a very remarkable person.' Further questions elicited from him that Mr. Kurtz was at present in charge of a trading post, a very important one, in the true ivory-country, at 'the very bottom of there. Sends in as much ivory as all the others put together . . .' He began to write again. The sick man was too ill to groan. The flies buzzed in a great peace.

"Suddenly there was a growing murmur of voices and a great tramping of feet. A caravan had come in. A violent babble of uncouth sounds burst out on the other side of the planks. All the carriers were speaking together, and in the midst of the uproar the lamentable voice of the chief agent was heard 'giving it up' tearfully for the twentieth time that day . . . He rose slowly. 'What a frightful row,' he said. He crossed the room gently to look at the sick man, and returning, said to me, 'He does not hear.' 'What! Dead?' I asked, startled. 'No, not yet,' he answered, with great composure. Then, alluding with a toss of the head to the tumult in the station yard, 'When one has got to make correct entries, one comes to hate those savages—hate them to the death.' He remained thoughtful for a moment. 'When you see Mr. Kurtz,' he went on, 'tell him from me that everything here'—he glanced at the desk—'is very satisfactory. I don't like to write to him—with those messengers of ours you never know who may get hold of your letter—at that Central Station.' He stared at me for a moment with his mild, bulging eyes. 'Oh, he will go far, very far,' he began again. 'He will be a somebody in the Administration before long. They, above—the Council in Europe, you know—mean him to be.'

"He turned to his work. The noise outside had ceased, and presently in going out I stopped at the door. In the steady buzz of flies the homeward-bound agent was lying flushed and insensible; the other, bent over his books, was making correct entries of perfectly correct transactions; and fifty feet below the doorstep I could see the still tree-tops of the grove of death.

"Next day I left that station at last, with a caravan of sixty men, for a two-hundred-mile tramp.

"No use telling you much about that. Paths, paths, everywhere; a stamped-in network of paths spreading over the empty land, through long grass, through burnt grass, through thickets, down and up chilly ravines, up and down stony hills ablaze with heat; and a solitude, a solitude, nobody, not a hut. The population had cleared out a long time ago. Well, if a lot of mysterious niggers armed with all kinds of fearful weapons suddenly took to travelling on the road between Deal and Gravesend, catching the yokels right and left to carry heavy loads for them, I fancy every farm and cottage thereabouts would get empty very soon. Only here the dwellings were gone, too. Still I passed through several abandoned villages. There's something pathetically childish in the ruins of grass walls. Day after day, with the stamp and shuffle of sixty pair of bare feet behind me, each pair under a 60-lb. load. Camp, cook, sleep, strike camp, march. Now and then a carrier dead in harness, at rest in the long grass near the path, with an empty water-gourd and his long staff lying by his side. A great silence around and above. Perhaps on some quiet night the tremor of far-off drums, sinking, swelling, a tremor vast, faint; a sound weird, appealing, suggestive, and wild—and perhaps with as profound a meaning as the sound of bells in a Christian country. Once a white man in an unbuttoned uniform, camping on the path with an armed escort of lank Zanzibaris, very hospitable and festive—not to say drunk. Was looking after the upkeep of the road, he declared. Can't say I saw any road or any upkeep, unless the body of a middle-aged negro, with a bullet-hole in the forehead, upon which I absolutely stumbled three miles farther on, may be considered as a permanent improvement. I had a white companion, too, not a bad chap, but rather too fleshy and with the exasperating habit of fainting on the hot hillsides, miles away from the least bit of shade and water. Annoying, you know, to hold your own coat like a parasol over a man's head while he is coming-to. I couldn't help asking him once what he meant by coming there at all. 'To make money, of course. What do you think?' he said, scornfully. Then he got fever, and had to be carried in a hammock slung under a pole. As he weighed sixteen stone I had no end of rows with the carriers. They jibbed, ran away, sneaked off with their loads in the night—quite a mutiny. So, one evening, I made a speech in English with gestures, not one of which was lost to the sixty pairs of eyes before me, and the next morning I started the hammock off in front all right. An hour afterwards I came upon the whole concern wrecked in a bush—man, hammock, groans, blankets, horrors. The heavy pole had skinned his poor nose. He was very anxious for me to kill somebody, but there wasn't the shadow of a carrier near. I remembered the old doctor,—'It would be interesting for science to watch the mental changes of individuals, on the spot.' I felt I was becoming scientifically interesting. However, all that is to no purpose. On the fifteenth day I came in sight of the big river again, and hobbled into the Central Station. It was on a backwater surrounded by scrub and forest, with a pretty border of smelly mud on one side, and on the three others enclosed by a crazy fence of rushes. A neglected gap was all the gate it had, and the first glance at the place was enough to let you see the flabby devil was running that show. White men with long staves in their hands appeared languidly from amongst the buildings, strolling up to take a look at me, and then retired out of sight somewhere. One of them, a stout, excitable chap with black moustaches, informed me with great volubility and many digressions, as soon as I told him who I was, that my steamer was at the bottom of the river. I was thunderstruck. What, how, why? Oh, it was 'all right.' The 'manager himself' was there. All quite correct. 'Everybody had behaved splendidly! splendidly!'—'You must,' he said in agitation, 'go and see the general manager at once. He is waiting!'

"I did not see the real significance of that wreck at once. I fancy I see it now, but I am not sure—not at all. Certainly the affair was too stupid—when I think of it—to be altogether natural. Still . . . But at the moment it presented itself simply as a confounded nuisance. The steamer was sunk. They had started two days before in a sudden hurry up the river with the manager on board, in charge of some volunteer skipper, and before they had been out three hours they tore the bottom out of her on stones, and she sank near the south bank. I asked myself what I was to do there, now my boat was lost. As a matter of fact, I had plenty to do in fishing my command out of the river. I had to set about it the very next day. That, and the repairs when I brought the pieces to the station, took some months.

"My first interview with the manager was curious. He did not ask me to sit down after my twenty-mile walk that morning. He was commonplace in complexion, in feature, in manners, and in voice. He was of middle size and of ordinary build. His eyes, of the usual blue, were perhaps remarkably cold, and he certainly could make his glance fall on one as trenchant and heavy as an axe. But even at these times the rest of his person seemed to disclaim the intention. Otherwise there was only an indefinable, faint expression of his lips, something stealthy—a smile—not a smile—I remember it, but I can't explain. It was unconscious, this smile was, though just after he had said something it got intensified for an instant. It came at the end of his speeches like a seal applied on the words to make the meaning of the commonest phrase appear absolutely inscrutable. He was a common trader, from his youth up employed in these parts—nothing more. He was obeyed, yet he inspired neither love nor fear. nor even respect. He inspired uneasiness. That was it! Uneasiness. Not a definite mistrust—just uneasiness—nothing more. You have no idea how effective such a . . . a . . . faculty can be. He had no genius for organizing, for initiative, or for order even. That was evident in such things as the deplorable state of the station. He had no learning, and no intelligence. His position had come to him—why? Perhaps because he was never ill . . . He had served three terms of three years out there . . . Because triumphant health in the general rout of constitutions is a kind of power in itself. When he went home on leave he rioted on a large scale— pompously. Jack ashore—with a difference—in externals only. This one could gather from his casual talk. He originated nothing, he could keep the routine going—that's all. But he was great. He was great by this little thing that it was impossible to tell what could control such a man. He never gave that secret away. Perhaps there was nothing within him. Such a suspicion made one pause—for out there there were no external checks. Once when various tropical diseases had laid low almost every 'agent' in the station, he was heard to say, 'Men who come out here should have no entrails.' He sealed the utterance with that smile of his, as though it had been a door opening into a darkness he had in his keeping. You fancied you had seen things—but the seal was on. When annoyed at meal-times by the constant quarrels of the white men about precedence, he or- dered an immense round table to be made, for which a special house had to be built. This was the station's mess-room. Where he sat was the first place—the rest were nowhere. One felt this to be his unalterable conviction. He was neither civil nor uncivil. He was quiet. He allowed his 'boy'—an overfed young Negro from the coast—to treat the white men, under his very eyes, with provoking insolence.

"He began to speak as soon as he saw me. I had been very long on the road. He could not wait. Had to start without me. The up- river stations had to be relieved. There had been so many delays al- ready that he did not know who was dead and who was alive, and how they got on—and so on, and so on. He paid no attention to my explanations and, playing with a stick of sealing-wax, repeated several times that the situation was 'very grave, very grave.' There were rumours that a very important station was in jeopardy, and its chief, Mr. Kurtz, was ill. Hoped it was not true. Mr. Kurtz was . . . I felt weary and irritable. Hang Kurtz, I thought. I interrupted him by saying I had heard of Mr. Kurtz on the coast. 'Ah! So they talk of him down there,' he murmured to himself. Then he began again, assuring me Mr. Kurtz was the best agent he had, an exceptional man, of the greatest importance to the Company; therefore I could understand his anxiety. He was, he said, 'very, very uneasy.' Certainly he fidgeted on his chair a good deal, exclaimed, 'Ah, Mr. Kurtz!', broke the stick of sealingwax and seemed dumbfounded by the accident. Next thing he wanted to know 'how long it would take to' . . . I interrupted him again. Being hungry, you know, and kept on my feet, too, I was getting savage. 'How could I tell?' I said. 'I hadn't even seen the wreck yet—some months, no doubt.' All this talk seemed to me so futile. 'Some months,' he said. 'Well, let us say three months before we can make a start. Yes. That ought to do the affair.' I flung out of his hut (he lived all alone in a clay hut with a sort of verandah) muttering to myself my opinion of him. He was a chattering idiot. Afterwards I took it back when it was borne in upon me startlingly with what extreme nicety he had estimated the time requisite for the 'affair.'

"I went to work the next day, turning, so to speak, my back on that station. In that way only it seemed to me I could keep my hold on the redeeming facts of life. Still, one must look about sometimes; and then I saw this station, these men strolling aimlessly about in the sunshine of the yard. I asked myself sometimes what it all meant. They wandered here and there with their absurd long staves in their hands, like a lot of faithless pilgrims bewitched inside a rotten fence. The word 'ivory' rang in the air, was whispered, was sighed. You would think they were praying to it. A taint of imbecile rapacity blew through it all, like a whiff from some corpse. By Jove! I've never seen anything so unreal in my life. And outside, the silent wilderness surrounding this cleared speck on the earth struck me as something great and invincible, like evil or truth, waiting patiently for the passing away of this fantastic invasion.

"Oh, these months! Well, never mind. Various things happened. One evening a grass shed full of calico, cotton print, beads, and I don't know what else, burst into a blaze so suddenly that you would have thought the earth had opened to let an avenging fire consume all that trash. I was smoking my pipe quietly by my dismantled steamer, and saw them all cutting capers in the light, with their arms lifted high, when the stout man with moustaches came tearing down to the river, a tin pail in his hand, assured me that everybody was 'behaving splendidly, splendidly,' dipped about a quart of water and tore back again. I noticed there was a hole in the bottom of his pail.

"I strolled up. There was no hurry. You see the thing had gone off like a box of matches. It had been hopeless from the very first. The flame had leaped high, driven everybody back, lighted up everything—and collapsed. The shed was already a heap of embers glowing fiercely. A nigger was being beaten near by. They said he had caused the fire in some way; be that as it may, he was screeching most horribly. I saw him, later, for several days, sitting in a bit of shade looking very sick and trying to recover himself: afterwards he arose and went out—and the wilderness without a sound took him into its bosom again. As I approached the glow from the dark I found myself at the back of two men, talking. I heard the name of Kurtz pronounced, then the words, 'take advantage of this unfortunate accident.' One of the men was the manager. I wished him a good evening. 'Did you ever see anything like it—eh? it is incredible,' he said, and walked off. The other man remained. He was a first-class agent, young, gentlemanly, a bit reserved, with a forked little beard and a hooked nose. He was stand-offish with the other agents, and they on their side said he was the manager's spy upon them. As to me, I had hardly ever spoken to him before. We got into talk, and by-and-by we strolled away from the hissing ruins. Then he asked me to his room, which was in the main building of the station. He struck a match, and I perceived that this young aristocrat had not only a silver-mounted dressing-case but also a whole candle all to himself. Just at that time the manager was the only man supposed to have any right to candles. Native mats covered the clay walls; a collection of spears, assegais, shields, knives was hung up in trophies. The business entrusted to this fellow was the making of bricks—so I had been informed; but there wasn't a fragment of a brick anywhere in the station, and he had been there more than a year—waiting. It seems he could not make bricks without something, I don't know what—straw maybe. Anyway, it could not be

* wilderness alive

found there, and as it was not likely to be sent from Europe, it did not appear clear to me what he was waiting for. An act of special creation perhaps. However, they were all waiting—all the sixteen or twenty pilgrims of them—for something; and upon my word it did not seem an uncongenial occupation, from the way they took it, though the only thing that ever came to them was disease—as far as I could see. They beguiled the time by backbiting and intriguing against each other in a foolish kind of way. There was an air of plotting about that station, but nothing came of it, of course. It was as unreal as everything else—as the philanthropic pretence of the whole concern, as their talk, as their government, as their show of work. The only real feeling was a desire to get appointed to a trading post where ivory was to be had, so that they could earn percentages. They intrigued and slandered and hated each other only on that account—but as to effectually lifting a little finger—oh, no. By heavens! there is something after all in the world allowing one man to steal a horse while another must not look at a halter. Steal a horse straight out. Very well. He has done it. Perhaps he can ride. But there is a way of looking at a halter that would provoke the most charitable of saints into a kick.

"I had no idea why he wanted to be sociable, but as we chatted in there it suddenly occurred to me the fellow was trying to get at something—in fact, pumping me. He alluded constantly to Europe, to the people I was supposed to know there—putting leading questions as to my acquaintances in the sepulchral city, and so on. His little eyes glittered like mica discs—with curiosity—though he tried to keep up a bit of superciliousness. At first I was astonished, but very soon I became awfully curious to see what he would find out from me. I couldn't possibly imagine what I had in me to make it worth his while. It was very pretty to see how he baffled himself, for in truth my body was full only of chills, and my head had nothing in it but that wretched steamboat business. It was evident he took me for a perfectly shameless prevaricator. At last he got angry, and to conceal a movement of furious annoyance, he yawned. I rose. Then I noticed a small sketch in oils, on a panel, representing a woman, draped and blindfolded, carrying a lighted torch. The background was sombre—almost black. The movement of the woman was stately, and the effect of the torch-light on the face was sinister.

"It arrested me, and he stood by civilly, holding an empty half-pint champagne bottle (medical comforts) with the candle stuck in it. To my question he said Mr. Kurtz had painted this—in this very station more than a year ago—while waiting for means to go to his trading post. 'Tell me, pray,' said I, 'who is this Mr. Kurtz?'

" 'The chief of the Inner Station,' he answered in a short tone, looking away. 'Much obliged,' I said, laughing. 'And you are the brickmaker of the Central Station. Everyone knows that.' He was silent for a while. 'He is a prodigy,' he said at last. 'He is an emissary of pity, and science, and progress, and devil knows what else. We want,' he began to declaim suddenly, 'for the guidance of the cause entrusted to us by Europe, so to speak, higher intelligence, wide sympathies, a singleness of purpose.' 'Who says that?' I asked. 'Lots of them,' he replied. 'Some even write that; and so *he* comes here, a special being, as you ought to know.' 'Why ought I to know?' I interrupted, really surprised. He paid no attention. 'Yes. Today he is chief of the best station, next year he will be assistant-manager, two years more and . . . but I daresay you know what he will be in two years' time. You are of the new gang—the gang of virtue. The same people who sent him specially also recommended you. Oh, don't say no. I've my own eyes to trust.' Light dawned upon me. My dear aunt's influential acquaintances were producing an unexpected effect upon that young man. I nearly burst into a laugh. 'Do you read the Company's confidential correspondence?' I asked. He hadn't a word to say. It was great fun. 'When Mr. Kurtz,' I continued, severely, 'is General Manager, you won't have the opportunity.'

"He blew the candle out suddenly, and we went outside. The moon had risen. Black figures strolled about listlessly, pouring water on the glow, whence proceeded a sound of hissing; steam ascended in the moonlight, the beaten nigger groaned somewhere. 'What a row the brute makes!' said the indefatigable man with the moustaches, appearing near us. 'Serve him right. Transgression—punishment—bang! Pitiless, pitiless. That's the only way. This will prevent all conflagrations for the future. I was just telling the manager . . .' He noticed my companion, and became crestfallen all at once. 'Not in bed yet,' he said, with a kind of servile heartiness; 'it's so natural. Ha! Danger—agitation.' He vanished. I went on to the river-side, and the other followed me. I heard a scathing murmur at my ear, 'Heap of muffs—go to.' The pilgrims could be seen in knots gesticulating, discussing. Several had still their staves in their hands. I verily believe they took these sticks to bed with them. Beyond the fence the forest stood up spectrally in the moonlight, and through the dim stir, through the faint sounds of that lamentable courtyard, the silence of the land went home to one's very heart—its mystery, its greatness, the amazing reality of its concealed life. The hurt nigger moaned feebly somewhere near by, and then fetched a deep sigh that made me mend my pace away from there. I felt a hand introducing itself under my arm. 'My dear sir,' said the fellow, 'I don't want to be misunderstood, and especially by you, who will see Mr. Kurtz long before I can have that pleasure. I wouldn't like him to get a false idea of my disposition . . .'

"I let him run on, this papier-mâché Mephistopheles, and it seemed to me that if I tried I could poke my forefinger through him, and would find nothing inside but a little loose dirt, maybe. He, don't you see, had been planning to be assistant-manager by-and-by under the present man, and I could see that the coming of that Kurtz had upset them both not a little. He talked precipitately, and I did not try to stop him. I had my shoulders against the wreck of my steamer, hauled up on the slope like a carcass of some big river animal. The smell of mud, of primeval mud, by Jove! was in my nostrils, the high stillness of primeval forest was before my eyes; there were shiny patches on the black creek. The moon had spread over everything a thin layer of silver—over the rank grass, over the mud, upon the wall of matted vegetation standing higher than the wall of a temple, over the great river I could see through a sombre gap glittering, glittering, as it flowed broadly by without a murmur. All this was great, expectant, mute, while the man jabbered about himself. I wondered whether the stillness on the face of the immensity looking at us two were meant as an appeal or as a menace. What were we who had strayed in here? Could we handle that dumb thing, or would it handle us? I felt how big, how confoundedly big, was that thing that couldn't talk, and perhaps was deaf as well. What was in there? I could see a little ivory coming out from there, and I had heard Mr. Kurtz was in there. I had heard enough about it, too— God knows! Yet somehow it didn't bring any image with it—no more than if I had been told an angel or a fiend was in there. I believed it in the same way one of you might believe there are inhabitants in the planet Mars. I knew once a Scotch sailmaker who was certain, dead sure, there were people in Mars. If you asked him for some idea how they looked and behaved, he would get shy and mutter something about 'walking on all fours.' If you as much as smiled, he would—though a man of sixty—offer to fight you. I would not have gone so far as to fight for Kurtz, but I went for him near enough to a lie. You know I hate, detest, and can't bear a lie, not because I am straighter than the rest of us, but simply because it appalls me. There is a taint of death, a flavour of mortality in lies—which is exactly what I hate and detest in the world—what I want to forget. It makes me miserable and sick, like biting something rotten would do. Temperament, I suppose. Well, I went near enough to it by letting the young fool there believe anything he liked to imagine as to my influence in Europe. I became in an instant as much of a pretence as the rest of the bewitched pilgrims. This simply because I had a notion it somehow would be of help to that Kurtz whom at the time I did not see—you understand. He was just a word for me. I did not see the man in the name any more than you do. Do you see him? Do you see the story? Do you see anything? It seems to me I am trying to tell you a dream—making a vain attempt, because no relation of a dream can convey the dream-sensation, that commingling of absurdity, surprise, and bewilderment in a tremor of struggling revolt, that notion of being captured by the incredible which is of the very essence of dreams . . ."

He was silent for a while.

". . . No, it is impossible; it is impossible to convey the life-sensation of any given epoch of one's existence—that which makes its truth, its meaning—its subtle and penetrating essence. It is impossible. We live, as we dream—alone . . ."

He paused again as if reflecting, then added—

"Of course in this you fellows see more than I could then. You see me, whom you know . . ."

It had become so pitch dark that we listeners could hardly see one another. For a long time already he, sitting apart, had been no more to us than a voice. There was not a word from anybody. The others might have been asleep, but I was awake. I listened, I listened on the watch for the sentence, for the word, that would give me the clue to the faint uneasiness inspired by this narrative that seemed to shape itself without human lips in the heavy night-air of the river.

". . . Yes—I let him run on," Marlow began again, "and think what he pleased about the powers that were behind me. I did! And there was nothing behind me! There was nothing but that wretched, old, mangled steamboat I was leaning against, while he talked fluently about 'the necessity for every man to get on.' 'And when one comes out here, you conceive, it is not to gaze at the moon.' Mr. Kurtz was a 'universal genius,' but even a genius would find it easier to work with 'adequate tools—intelligent men.' He did not make bricks—why, there was a physical impossibility in the way—as I was well aware; and if he did secretarial work for the manager, it was because 'no sensible man rejects wantonly the confidence of his superiors.' Did I see it? I saw it. What more did I want? What I really wanted was rivets, by heaven! Rivets. To get on with the work—to stop the hole. Rivets I wanted. There were cases of them down at the coast—cases—piled up—burst—split! You kicked a loose rivet at every second step in that station yard on the hillside. Rivets had rolled into the grove of death. You could fill your pockets with rivets for the trouble of stooping down—and there wasn't one rivet to be found where it was wanted. We had plates that would do, but nothing to fasten them with. And every week the messenger, a lone negro, letter-bag on shoulder and staff in hand, left our station for the coast. And several times a week a coast caravan came in with trade goods—ghastly glazed calico that made you shudder only to look at it, glass beads value about a penny a quart, confounded spotted cotton handkerchiefs. And no rivets. Three carriers could have brought all that was wanted to set that steamboat afloat.

"He was becoming confidential now, but I fancy my unresponsive attitude must have exasperated him at last, for he judged it necessary to inform me he feared neither God nor devil, let alone any mere man. I said I could see that very well, but what I wanted was a certain quantity of rivets—and rivets were what really Mr. Kurtz wanted, if he had only known it. Now letters went to the coast every week ... 'My dear sir,' he cried, 'I write from dictation.' I demanded rivets. There was a way—for an intelligent man. He changed his manner; became very cold, and suddenly began to talk about a hippopotamus; wondered whether sleeping on board the steamer (I stuck to my salvage night and day) I wasn't disturbed. There was an old hippo that had the bad habit of getting out on the bank and roaming at night over the station grounds. The pilgrims used to turn out in a body and empty every rifle they could lay hands on at him. Some even had sat up o' nights for him. All this energy was wasted, though. 'That animal has a charmed life,' he said; 'but you can say this only of brutes in this country. No man—you apprehend me?—no man here bears a charmed life.' He stood there for a moment in the moonlight with his delicate hooked nose set a little askew, and his mica eyes glittering without a wink, then, with a curt Good-night, he strode off. I could see he was disturbed and considerably puzzled, which made me feel more hopeful than I had been for days. It was a great comfort to turn from that chap to my influential friend, the battered, twisted ruined, tin-pot steamboat. I clambered on board. She rang under my feet like an empty Huntley & Palmers biscuit-tin kicked along a gutter; she was nothing so solid in make, and rather less pretty in shape, but I had expended enough hard work on her to make me love her. No influential friend would have served me better. She had given me a chance to come out a bit—to find out what I could do. No, I don't like work. I had rather laze about and think of all the fine things that can be done. I don't like work,—no man does—but I like what is in the work,—the chance to find yourself. Your own reality—for yourself, not for others—what no other man can ever know. They can only see the mere show, and never can tell what it really means.

"I was not surprised to see somebody sitting aft, on the deck, with his legs dangling over the mud. You see I rather chummed with the few mechanics there were in that station, whom the other pilgrims naturally despised—on account of their imperfect manners, I suppose. This was the foreman—a boiler-maker by trade—a good worker. He was a lank, bony, yellow-faced man, with big intense eyes. His aspect was worried, and his head was as bald as the palm of my hand; but his hair in falling seemed to have stuck to his chin, and had prospered in the new locality, for his beard hung down to his waist. He was a widower with six young children (he had left them in charge of a sister of his to come out there), and the passion of his life was pigeon-flying. He was an enthusiast and a connoisseur. He would rave about pigeons. After work hours he used sometimes to come over from his hut for a talk about his children and his pigeons; at work, when he had to crawl in the mud under the bottom of the steamboat, he would tie up that beard of his in a kind of white serviette he brought for the purpose. It had loops to go over his ears. In the evening he could be seen squatted on the bank rinsing that wrapper in the creek with great care, then spreading it solemnly on a bush to dry.

"I slapped him on the back and shouted 'We shall have rivets!' He scrambled to his feet exclaiming 'No! Rivets!' as though he couldn't believe his ears. Then in a low voice, 'You . . . eh?' I don't know why we behaved like lunatics. I put my finger to the side of my nose and nodded mysteriously. 'Good for you!' he cried, snapped his fingers above his head, lifting one foot. I tried a jig. We capered on the iron deck. A frightful clatter came out of that hulk, and the virgin forest on the other bank of the creek sent it back in a thundering roll upon the sleeping station. It must have made some of the pilgrims sit up in their hovels. A dark figure obscured the lighted doorway of the manager's hut, vanished, then, a second or so after, the doorway itself vanished, too. We stopped, and the silence driven away by the stamping of our feet flowed back again from the recesses of the land. The great wall of vegetation, an exuberant and entangled mass of trunks, branches, leaves, boughs, festoons, motionless in the moonlight, was like a rioting invasion of soundless life, a rolling wave of plants, piled up, crested, ready to topple over the creek, to sweep every little man of us out of his little existence. And it moved not. A deadened burst of mighty splashes and snorts reached us from afar, as though an ichthyosaurus had been taking a bath of glitter in the great river. 'After all,' said the boiler-maker in a reasonable tone, 'why shouldn't we get the rivets?' Why not, indeed! I did not know of any reason why we shouldn't. 'They'll come in three weeks,' I said, confidently.

"But they didn't. Instead of rivets there came an invasion, an infliction, a visitation. It came in sections during the next three weeks, each section headed by a donkey carrying a white man in new clothes and tan shoes, bowing from that elevation right and left to the impressed pilgrims. A quarrelsome band of footsore sulky niggers trod on the heels of the donkey; a lot of tents, camp-stools, tin boxes, white cases, brown bales would be shot down in the courtyard, and the air of mystery would deepen a little over the muddle of the station. Five such instalments came, with their absurd air of disorderly flight with the loot of innumerable outfit shops and provision stores, that, one would think, they were lugging, after a raid, into the wilderness for equitable division. It was an inextricable mess of things decent in themselves but that human folly made look like spoils of thieving.

"This devoted band called itself the Eldorado Exploring Expedition, and I believe they were sworn to secrecy. Their talk, however, was the talk of sordid buccaneers: it was reckless without hardihood, greedy without audacity, and cruel without courage; there was not an atom of foresight or of serious intention in the whole batch of them, and they did not seem aware these things are wanted for the work of the world. To tear treasure out of the bowels of the land was their desire, with no more moral purpose at the back of it than there is in burglars breaking into a safe. Who paid the expenses of the noble enterprise I don't know; but the uncle of our manager was leader of that lot.

"In exterior he resembled a butcher in a poor neighbourhood, and his eyes had a look of sleepy cunning. He carried his fat paunch with ostentation on his short legs, and during the time his gang infested the station spoke to no one but his nephew. You could see these two roaming about all day long with their heads close together in an everlasting confab.

"I had given up worrying myself about the rivets. One's capacity for that kind of folly is more limited than you would suppose. I said Hang!—and let things slide. I had plenty of time for meditation, and now and then I would give some thought to Kurtz. I wasn't very interested in him. No. Still, I was curious to see whether this man, who had come out equipped with moral ideas of some sort, would climb to the top after all and how he would set about his work when there."

II

"One evening as I was lying flat on the deck of my steamboat, I heard voices approaching—and there were the nephew and the uncle strolling along the bank. I laid my head on my arm again, and had nearly lost myself in a doze, when somebody said in my ear, as it were: 'I am as harmless as a little child, but I don't like to be dictated to. Am I the manager—or am I not? I was ordered to send him there. It's incredible.' . . . I became aware that the two were standing on the shore alongside the forepart of the steamboat, just below my head. I did not move; it did not occur to me to move: I was sleepy. 'It *is* unpleasant,' grunted the uncle. 'He has asked the Administration to be sent there,' said the other, 'with the idea of showing what he could do; and I was instructed accordingly. Look at the influence that man must have. Is it not frightful?' They both agreed it was frightful, then made several bizarre remarks: 'Make rain and fine weather—one man—the Council—by the nose'—bits of absurd sentenes that got the better of my drowsiness, so that I had pretty near the whole of my wits about me when the uncle said, 'The climate may do away with this difficulty for you. Is he alone there?' 'Yes,' answered the manager; 'he sent his assistant down the river with a note to me in these terms: "Clear this poor devil out of the country, and don't bother sending more of that sort. I had rather be alone than have the kind of men you can dispose of with me." It was more than a year ago. Can you imagine such impudence!' 'Anything since then?' aksed the other, hoarsely. 'Ivory,' jerked the nephew; 'lots of it—prime sort—lots—most annoying, from him.' 'And with that?' questioned the heavy rumble. 'Invoice,' was the reply fired out, so to speak. Then silence. They had been talking about Kurtz.

"I was broad awake by this time, but, lying perfectly at ease, remained still, having no inducement to change my position. 'How did that ivory come all this way?' growled the elder man, who seemed very vexed. The other explained that it had come with a fleet of canoes in charge of an English half-caste clerk Kurtz had with him; that Kurtz had apparently intended to return himself, the station being by that time bare of goods and stores, but after coming three hundred miles, had suddenly decided to go back, which he started to do alone in a small dugout with four paddlers, leaving the half-caste to continue down the river with the ivory. The two fellows there seemed astounded at anybody attempting such a thing. They were at a loss for an adequate motive. As to me, I seemed to see Kurtz for the first time. It was a distinct glimpse: the dugout, four paddling savages, and the lone white man turning his back suddenly on the headquarters, on relief, on thoughts of home—perhaps; setting his face towards the depths of the wilderness, towards his empty and desolate station. I did not know the motive. Perhaps he was just simply a fine fellow who stuck to his work for its own sake. His name, you understand, had not been pronounced once. He was 'that man.' The half-caste, who, as far as I could see, had conducted a difficult trip with great prudence and pluck, was invariably alluded to as 'that scoundrel.' The 'scoundrel' had reported that the 'man' had been very ill—had recovered imperfectly . . . The two below me moved away then a few paces, and strolled back and forth at some little distance. I heard: 'Military post—doctor—two hundred miles—quite alone now—unavoidable delays—nine months—no news—strange rumours.' They approached again, just as the manager was saying, 'No one, as far as I know, unless a species of wandering trader—a pestilential fellow, snapping ivory from the natives.' Who was it they were talking about now? I gathered in snatches that this was some man supposed to be in Kurtz's district, and of whom the manager did not approve. 'We will not be free from unfair competition till one of these fellows is hanged for an example,' he said. 'Certainly,' grunted the other; 'get him hanged! Why not? Anything—anything can be done in this country. That's what I say; nobody here, you understand, *here*, can endanger your position. And why? You stand the climate—you outlast them all. The danger is in Europe; but there before I left I took care to—' They moved off and whispered, then their voices rose again. 'The extraordinary series of delays is not my fault. I did my best.' The fat man sighed. 'Very sad.' 'And the pestiferous absurdity of his talk,' continued the other; 'he bothered me enough when he was here. "Each station should be like a beacon on the road towards better things, a centre for trade of course, but also for humanizing, improving, instructing." Conceive you—that ass! And he wants to be manager! No, it's—' Here he got choked by excessive indignation, and I lifted my head the least bit. I was surprised to see how near they were—right under me. I could have spat upon their hats. They were looking on the ground, absorbed in thought. The manager was switching his leg with a slender twig: his sagacious relative lifted his head. 'You have been well since you came out this time?' he asked. The other gave a start. 'Who? I? Oh! Like a charm—like a charm. But the rest—oh, my goodness! All sick. They die so quick, too, that I haven't the time to send them out of the country—it's incredible!' 'H'm. Just so,' grunted the uncle. 'Ah! my boy, trust to this—I say, trust to this.' I saw him extend his short flipper of an arm for a gesture that took in the forest, the creek, the mud, the river—seemed to beckon with a dishonouring flourish before the sunlit face of the land a treacherous appeal to the lurking death, to the hidden evil, to the profound darkness of its heart. It was so startling that I leaped to my feet and looked back at the edge of the forest, as though I had expected an answer of some sort to that black display of confidence. You know the foolish notions that come to one sometimes. The high stillness confronted these two figures with its ominous patience, waiting for the passing away of a fantastic invasion.

"They swore aloud together—out of sheer fright, I believe—then pretending not to know anything of my existence, turned back to the station. The sun was low; and leaning forward side by side, they seemed to be tugging painfully uphill their two ridiculous shadows of unequal length, that trailed behind them slowly over the tall grass without bending a single blade.

"In a few days the Eldorado Expedition went into the patient wilderness, that closed upon it as the sea closes over a diver. Long afterwards the news came that all the donkeys were dead. I know nothing as to the fate of the less valuable animals. They, no doubt, like the rest of us, found what they deserved. I did not inquire. I was then rather excited at the prospect of meeting Kurtz very soon. When I say very soon I mean it comparatively. It was just two months from the day we left the creek when we came to the bank below Kurtz's station.

"Going up that river was like travelling back to the earliest beginnings of the world, when vegetation rioted on the earth and the big trees were kings. An empty stream, a great silence, an impenetrable forest. The air was warm, thick, heavy, sluggish. There was no joy in the brilliance of sunshine. The long stretches of the waterway ran on, deserted, into the gloom of overshadowed distances. On silvery sandbanks hippos and alligators sunned themselves side by side. The broadening waters flowed through a mob of wooded islands; you lost your way on that river as you would in a desert, and butted all day long against shoals, trying to find the channel, till you thought yourself bewitched and cut off for ever from everything you had known once—somewhere—far away—in another existence perhaps. There were moments when one's past came back to one, as it will sometimes when you have not a moment to spare to yourself; but it came in the shape of an unrestful and noisy dream, remembered with wonder amongst the overwhelming realities of this strange world of plants, and water, and silence. And this stillness of life did not in the least resemble a peace. It was the stillness of an implacable force brooding over an inscrutable intention. It looked at you with a vengeful aspect. I got used to it afterwards; I did not see it any more; I had no time. I had to keep guessing at the channel; I had to discern, mostly by inspiration, the signs of hidden banks; I watched for sunken stones; I was learning to clap my teeth smartly before my heart flew out, when I shaved by a fluke some infernal sly old snag that would have ripped the life out of the tin-pot steamboat and drowned all the pilgrims; I had to keep a look-out for the signs of dead wood we could cut up in the night for next day's steaming. When you have to attend to things of that sort, to the mere incidents of the surface, the reality—the reality, I tell you— fades. The inner truth is hidden—luckily, luckily. But I felt it all the same; I felt often its mysterious stillness watching me at my monkey tricks, just as it watches you fellows performing on your respective tight-ropes for—what is it? half-a-crown a tumble—"

"Try to be civil, Marlow," growled a voice, and I knew there was at least one listener awake besides myself.

"I beg your pardon. I forgot the heartache which makes up the rest of the price. And indeed what does the price matter, if the trick be well done? You do your tricks very well. And I didn't do badly either, since I managed not to sink that steamboat on my first trip. It's a wonder to me yet. Imagine a blindfolded man set to drive a van over a bad road. I sweated and shivered over that business considerably, I can tell you. After all, for a seaman, to scrape the bottom of the thing that's supposed to float all the time under his care is the unpardonable sin. No one may know of it, but you never forget the thump—eh? A blow on the very heart. You remember it, you dream of it, you wake up at night and think of it—years after—and go hot and cold all over. I don't pretend to say that steamboat floated all the time. More than once she had to wade for a bit, with twenty cannibals splashing around and pushing. We had enlisted some of these chaps on the way for a crew. Fine fellows—cannibals—in their place. They were men one could work with, and I am grateful to them. And, after all, they did not eat each other before my face: they had brought along a provision of hippo-meat which went rotten, and made the mystery of the wilderness stink in my nostrils. Phoo!

I can sniff it now. I had the manager on board and three or four pilgrims with their staves—all complete. Sometimes we came upon a station close by the bank, clinging to the skirts of the unknown, and the white men rushing out of a tumbledown hovel, with great gestures of joy and surprise and welcome, seemed very strange—had the appearance of being held there captive by a spell. The word ivory would ring in the air for a while—and on we went again into the silence, along empty reaches, round the still bends, between the high walls of our winding way, reverberating in hollow claps the ponderous beat of the stern-wheel. Trees, trees, millions of trees, massive, immense, running up high; and at their foot, hugging the bank against the stream, crept the little begrimed steamboat, like a sluggish beetle crawling on the floor of a lofty portico. It made you feel very small, very lost, and yet it was not altogether depressing, that feeling. After all, if you were small, the grimy beetle crawled on—which was just what you wanted it to do. Where the pilgrims imagined it crawled to I don't know. To some place where they expected to get something, I bet! For me it crawled towards Kurtz—exclusively; but when the steam-pipes started leaking we crawled very slow. The reaches opened before us and closed behind, as if the forest had stepped leisurely across the water to bar the way for our return. We penetrated deeper and deeper into the heart of darkness. It was very quiet there. At night sometimes the roll of drums behind the curtain of trees would run up the river and remain sustained faintly, as if hovering in the air high over our heads, till the first break of day. Whether it meant war, peace, or prayer we could not tell. The dawns were heralded by the descent of a chill stillness; the wood-cutters slept, their fires burned low; the snapping of a twig would make you start. We were wanderers on prehistoric earth, on an earth that wore the aspect of an unknown planet. We could have fancied ourselves the first of men taking possession of an accursed inheritance, to be subdued at the cost of profound anguish and of excessive toil. But suddenly, as we struggled round a bend, there would be a glimpse of rush walls, of peaked grass-roofs, a burst of yells, a whirl of black limbs, a mass of hands clapping, of feet stamping, of bodies swaying, of eyes rolling, under the droop of heavy and motionless foliage. The steamer toiled along slowly on the edge of a black and incomprehensible frenzy. The prehistoric man was cursing us, praying to us, welcoming us— who could tell? We were cut off from the comprehension of our surroundings; we glided past like phantoms, wondering and secretly appalled, as sane men would be before an enthusiastic outbreak in a madhouse. We could not understand because we were too far and could not remember, because we were travelling in the night of first ages, of those ages that are gone, leaving hardly a sign—and no memories.

"The earth seemed unearthly. We are accustomed to look upon the shackled form of a conquered monster, but there—there you could look at a thing monstrous and free. It was unearthly, and the men were—No, they were not inhuman. Well, you know, that was the worst of it—this suspicion of their not being inhuman. It would come slowly to one. They howled and leaped, and spun, and made horrid faces; but what thrilled you was just the thought of their humanity—like yours—the thought of your remote kinship with this wild and passionate uproar. Ugly. Yes, it was ugly enough; but if you were man enough you would admit to yourself that there was in you just the faintest trace of a response to the terrible frankness of that noise, a dim suspicion of there being a meaning in it which you—you so remote from the night of first ages—could comprehend. And why not? The mind of man is capable of anything— because everything is in it, all the past as well as all the future. What was there after all? Joy, fear, sorrow, devotion, valour, rage—who can tell?—but truth—truth stripped of its cloak of time. Let the fool gape and shudder—the man knows, and can look on without a wink. But he must at least be as much of a man as these on the shore. He must meet that truth with his own true stuff—with his own inborn strength. Principles won't do. Acquisitions, clothes, pretty rags—rags that would fly off at the first good shake. No; you want a deliberate belief. An appeal to me in this fiendish row—is there? Very well; I hear; I admit, but I have a voice, too, and for good or evil mine is the speech that cannot be silenced. Of course, a fool, what with sheer fright and fine sentiments, is always safe. Who's that grunting? You wonder I didn't go ashore for a howl and a dance? Well, no—I didn't. Fine sentiments, you say? Fine sentiments, be hanged! I had no time. I had to mess about with white-lead and strips of woollen blanket helping to put bandages on those leaky steam-pipes—I tell you. I had to watch the steering, and circumvent those snags, and get the tin-pot along by hook or by crook. There was surface-truth enough in these things to save a wiser man. And between whiles I had to look after the savage who was fireman. He was an improved specimen; he could fire up a vertical boiler. He was there below me, and, upon my word, to look at him was as edifying as seeing a dog in a parody of breeches and a feather hat, walking on his hind-legs. A few months of training had done for that really fine chap. He squinted at the steam-gauge and at the water-gauge with an evident effort of intrepidity—and he had filed teeth, too, the poor devil, and the wool of his pate shaved into queer patterns, and three ornamental scars on each of his cheeks. He ought to have been clapping his hands and stamping his feet on the bank, instead of which he was hard at work, a thrall to strange witchcraft, full of improving knowledge. He was useful because he had been instructed; and what he knew was this—that should the water in that transparent thing disappear, the evil spirit inside the boiler would get angry through the greatness of his thirst, and take a terrible vengeance. So he sweated and fired up and watched the glass fearfully (with an impromptu charm, made of rags, tied to his arm, and a piece of polished bone, as big as a watch, stuck flatways through his lower lip), while the wooded banks slipped past us slowly, the short noise was left behind, the interminable miles of silence—and we crept on, towards Kurtz. But the snags were thick, the water was treacherous and shallow, the boiler seemed indeed to have a sulky devil in it, and thus neither that fireman nor I had any time to peer into our creepy thoughts.

"Some fifty miles below the Inner Station we came upon a hut of reeds, an inclined and melancholy pole, with the unrecognizable tatters of what had been a flag of some sort flying from it, and a neatly stacked wood-pile. This was unexpected. We came to the bank, and on the stack of firewood found a flat piece of board with

some faded pencil-writing on it. When deciphered it said: 'Wood
for you. Hurry up. Approach cautiously.' There was a signature, but
it was illegible—not Kurtz—a much longer word. Hurry up.
Where? Up the river? 'Approach cautiously.' We had not done so.
But the warning could not have been meant for the place where it
could be only found after approach. Something was wrong above.
But what—and how much? That was the question. We commented
adversely upon the imbecility of that telegraphic style. The bush
around said nothing, and would not let us look very far, either. A
torn curtain of red twill hung in the doorway of the hut, and
flapped sadly in our faces. The dwelling was dismantled; but we
could see a white man had lived there not very long ago. There remained a rude table—a plank on two posts; a heap of rubbish reposed in a dark corner, and by the door I picked up a book. It had
lost its covers, and the pages had been thumbed into a state of extremely dirty softness; but the back had been lovingly stitched
afresh with white cotton thread, which looked clean yet. It was an
extraordinary find. Its title was, *An Inquiry into some Points of Seaman-
ship*, by a man, Tower, Towson—some such name—Master in His
Majesty's Navy. The matter looked dreary reading enough, with il-
lustrative diagrams and repulsive tables of figures, and the copy was
sixty years old. I handled this amazing antiquity with the greatest
possible tenderness, lest it should dissolve in my hands. Within,
Towson or Towser was inquiring earnestly into the breaking strain
of ships' chains and tackle, and other such matters. Not a very en-
thralling book; but at the first glance you could see there a singleness of intention, an honest concern for the right way of going to
work, which made these humble pages, thought out so many years
ago, luminous with another than a professional light. The simple
old sailor, with his talk of chains and purchases, made me forget the
jungle and the pilgrims in a delicious sensation of having come
upon something unmistakably real. Such a book being there was
wonderful enough; but still more astounding were the notes pen-
cilled in the margin, and plainly referring to the text. I couldn't believe my eyes! They were in cipher! Yes, it looked like cipher. Fancy
a man lugging with him a book of that description into this nowhere

and studying it—and making notes—in cipher at that! It was an extravagant mystery.

"I had been dimly aware for some time of a worrying noise, and when I lifted my eyes I saw the wood-pile was gone, and the manager, aided by all the pilgrims, was shouting at me from the riverside. I slipped the book into my pocket. I assure you to leave off reading was like tearing myself away from the shelter of an old and solid friendship.

"I started the lame engine ahead. 'It must be this miserable trader—this intruder,' exclaimed the manager, looking back malevolently at the place we had left. 'He must be English,' I said. 'It will not save him from getting into trouble if he is not careful,' muttered the manager darkly. I observed with assumed innocence that no man was safe from trouble in this world.

"The current was more rapid now, the steamer seemed at her last gasp, the stern-wheel flopped languidly, and I caught myself listening on tiptoe for the next beat of the float, for in sober truth I expected the wretched thing to give up every moment. It was like watching the last flickers of a life. But still we crawled. Sometimes I would pick out a tree a little way ahead to measure our progress towards Kurtz by, but I lost it invariably before we got abreast. To keep the eyes so long on one thing was too much for human patience. The manager displayed a beautiful resignation. I fretted and fumed and took to arguing with myself whether or no I would talk openly with Kurtz; but before I could come to any conclusion it occurred to me that my speech or my silence, indeed any action of mine, would be a mere futility. What did it matter what anyone knew or ignored? What did it matter who was manager? One gets sometimes such a flash of insight. The essentials of this affair lay deep under the surface, beyond my reach, and beyond my power of meddling.

"Towards the evening of the second day we judged ourselves about eight miles from Kurtz's station. I wanted to push on; but the manager looked grave, and told me the navigation up there was so dangerous that it would be advisable, the sun being very low already, to wait where we were till next morning. Moreover, he pointed out that if the warning to approach cautiously were to be followed, we must approach in daylight—not at dusk, or in the dark. This was sensible enough. Eight miles meant nearly three hours' steaming for us, and I could also see suspicious ripples at the upper end of the reach. Nevertheless, I was annoyed beyond expression at the delay, and most unreasonably, too, since one night more could not matter much after so many months. As we had plenty of wood, and caution was the word, I brought up in the middle of the stream. The reach was narrow, straight, with high sides like a railway cutting. The dusk came gliding into it long before the sun had set. The current ran smooth and swift, but a dumb immobility sat on the banks. The living trees, lashed together by the creepers and every living bush of the undergrowth, might have been changed into stone, even to the slenderest twig, to the lightest leaf. It was not sleep—it seemed unnatural. Like a state of trance. Not the faintest sound of any kind could be heard. You looked on amazed, and began to suspect yourself of being deaf—then the night came suddenly, and struck you blind as well. About three in the morning some large fish leaped, and the loud splash made me jump as though a gun had been fired. When the sun rose there was a white fog, very warm and clammy, and more blinding than the night. It did not shift or drive; it was just there, standing all round you like something solid. At eight or nine, perhaps, it lifted as a shutter lifts. We had a glimpse of the towering multitude of trees, of the immense matted jungle, with the blazing little ball of the sun hanging over it—all perfectly still—and then the white shutter came down again, smoothly, as if sliding in greased grooves. I ordered the chain, which we had begun to heave in, to be paid out again. Before it stopped running with a muffled rattle, a cry, a very loud cry, as of infinite desolation, soared slowly in the opaque air. It ceased. A complaining clamour, modulated in savage discords, filled our ears. The sheer unexpectedness of it made my hair stir under my cap. I don't know how it struck the others: to me it seemed as though the mist itself had screamed, so suddenly, and apparently from all sides at once, did this tumultuous and mournful uproar arise. It culminated in a hurried outbreak of almost intolerably excessive shrieking, which stopped short, leaving us stiffened in a variety of silly attitudes, and obstinately listening to the nearly as appalling and excessive silence. 'Good God! What is the meaning—' stammered at my elbow one of the pilgrims,—a little fat man, with sandy hair and red whiskers, who wore side-spring boots, and pink pyjamas tucked into his socks. Two others remained openmouthed a whole minute, then dashed into the little cabin, to rush out incontinently and stand darting scared glances, with Winchesters at 'ready' in their hands. What we could see was just the steamer we were on, her outlines blurred as though she had been on the point of dissolving, and a misty strip of water, perhaps two feet broad, around her—and that was all. The rest of the world was nowhere, as far as our eyes and ears were concerned. Just nowhere. Gone, disappeared; swept off without leaving a whisper or a shadow behind.

"I went forward, and ordered the chain to be hauled in short, so as to be ready to trip the anchor and move the steamboat at once if necessary. 'Will they attack?' whispered an awed voice. 'We will be all butchered in this fog,' murmured another. The faces twitched with the strain, the hands trembled slightly, the eyes forgot to wink. It was very curious to see the contrast of expressions of the white men and of the black fellows of our crew, who were as much strangers to that part of the river as we, though their homes were only eight hundred miles away. The whites, of course greatly discomposed, had besides a curious look of being painfully shocked by such an outrageous row. The others had an alert, naturally interested expression; but their faces were essentially quiet, even those of the one or two who grinned as they hauled at the chain. Several exchanged short, grunting phrases, which seemed to settle the matter to their satisfaction. Their headman, a young, broad-chested black, severely draped in dark-blue fringed cloths, with fierce nostrils and his hair all done up artfully in oily ringlets, stood near me. 'Aha!' I said, just for good fellowship's sake. 'Catch 'im,' he snapped, with a bloodshot widening of his eyes and a flash of sharp teeth— 'catch 'im. Give 'im to us.' 'To you, eh?' I asked; 'what would you do with them?' 'Eat 'im!' he said, curtly, and, leaning his elbow on the rail, looked out into the fog in a dignified and profoundly pensive attitude. I would no doubt have been properly horrified, had it not occurred to me that he and his chaps must be very hungry: that they must have been growing increasingly hungry for at least this month past. They had been engaged for six months (I don't think a single one of them had any clear idea of time, as we at the end of countless ages have. They still belonged to the beginnings of time—had no inherited experience to teach them, as it were), and, of course, as long as there was a piece of paper written over in accordance with some farcical law or other made down the river, it didn't enter anybody's head to trouble how they would live. Certainly they had brought with them some rotten hippo-meat, which couldn't have lasted very long, anyway, even if the pilgrims hadn't, in the midst of a shocking hullabaloo, thrown a considerable quantity of it overboard. It looked like a high-handed proceeding; but it was really a case of legitimate self-defence. You can't breathe dead hippo waking, sleeping, and eating, and at the same time keep your precarious grip on existence. Besides that, they had given them every week three pieces of brass wire, each about nine inches long; and the theory was they were to buy their provisions with that currency in river-side villages. You can see how *that* worked. There were either no villages, or the people were hostile, or the director, who like the rest of us fed out of tins, with an occasional old he-goat thrown in, didn't want to stop the steamer for some more or less recondite reason. So, unless they swallowed the wire itself, or made loops of it to snare the fishes with, I don't see what good their extravagant salary could be to them. I must say it was paid with a regularity worthy of a large and honourable trading company. For the rest, the only thing to eat—though it didn't look eatable in the least—I saw in their possession was a few lumps of some stuff like half-cooked dough, of a dirty lavender colour, they kept wrapped in leaves, and now and then swallowed a piece of, but so small that it seemed done more for the looks of the thing than for any serious purpose of sustenance. Why in the name of all the gnawing devils of hunger they didn't go for us—they were thirty to five—and have a good tuck in

for once, amazes me now when I think of it. They were big powerful men, with not much capacity to weigh the consequences, with
courage, with strength, even yet, though their skins were no longer
glossy and their muscles no longer hard. And I saw that something
restraining, one of those human secrets that baffle probability, had
come into play there. I looked at them with a swift quickening of
interest—not because it occurred to me I might be eaten by them
before very long, though I own to you that just then I perceived—
in a new light, as it were—how unwholesome the pilgrims looked,
and I hoped, yes, I positively hoped, that my aspect was not so—
what shall I say?—so—unappetizing: a touch of fantastic vanity
which fitted well with the dream-sensation that pervaded all my
days at that time. Perhaps I had a little fever, too. One can't live with
one's finger everlastingly on one's pulse. I had often 'a little fever,'
or a little touch of other things—the playful paw-strokes of the
wilderness, the preliminary trifling before the more serious onslaught which came in due course. Yes; I looked at them as you
would on any human being, with a curiosity of their impulses, motives, capacities, weaknesses, when brought to the test of an inexorable physical necessity. Restraint! What possible restraint? Was it
superstition, disgust, patience, fear—or some kind of primitive honour? No fear can stand up to hunger, no patience can wear it out,
disgust simply does not exist where hunger is; and as to superstition, beliefs, and what you may call principles, they are less than
chaff in a breeze. Don't you know the devilry of lingering starvation, its exasperating torment, its black thoughts, its sombre and
brooding ferocity? Well, I do. It takes a man all his inborn strength
to fight hunger properly. It's really easier to face bereavement, dis-
honour, and the perdition of one's soul—than this kind of prolonged hunger. Sad, but true. And these chaps, too, had no earthly
reason for any kind of scruple. Restraint! I would just as soon have
expected restraint from a hyena prowling amongst the corpses of a
battlefield. But there was the fact facing me—the fact dazzling, to
be seen, like the foam on the depths of the sea, like a ripple on an
unfathomable enigma, a mystery greater—when I thought of it—

IMPERIAL THOUGHTS?

than the curious, inexplicable note of desperate grief in this savage clamour that had swept by us on the river-bank, behind the blind whiteness of the fog.

"Two pilgrims were quarrelling in hurried whispers as to which bank. 'Left.' 'No, no; how can you? Right, right, of course.' 'It is very serious,' said the manager's voice behind me; 'I would be desolated if anything should happen to Mr. Kurtz before we came up.' I looked at him, and had not the slightest doubt he was sincere. He was just the kind of man who would wish to preserve appearances. That was his restraint. But when he muttered something about going on at once, I did not even take the trouble to answer him. I knew, and he knew, that it was impossible. Were we to let go our hold of the bottom, we would be absolutely in the air—in space. We wouldn't be able to tell where we were going to—whether up or down stream, or across—till we fetched against one bank or the other—and then we wouldn't know at first which it was. Of course I made no move. I had no mind for a smash-up. You couldn't imagine a more deadly place for a shipwreck. Whether drowned at once or not, we were sure to perish speedily in one way or another. 'I authorize you to take all the risks,' he said, after a short silence. 'I refuse to take any,' I said, shortly; which was just the answer he expected, though its tone might have surprised him. 'Well, I must defer to your judgement. You are captain,' he said, with marked civility. I turned my shoulder to him in sign of my appreciation, and looked into the fog. How long would it last? It was the most hopeless look-out. The approach to this Kurtz grubbing for ivory in the wretched bush was beset by as many dangers as though he had been an enchanted princess sleeping in a fabulous castle. 'Will they attack, do you think?' asked the manager, in a confidential tone.

"I did not think they would attack, for several obvious reasons. The thick fog was one. If they left the bank in their canoes they would get lost in it, as we would be if we attempted to move. Still, I had also judged the jungle of both banks quite impenetrable—and yet eyes were in it, eyes that had seen us. The river-side bushes were certainly very thick; but the undergrowth behind was evidently penetrable. However, during the short lift I had seen no canoes anywhere in the reach—certainly not abreast of the steamer. But what made the idea of attack inconceivable to me was the nature of the noise—of the cries we had heard. They had not the fierce character boding of immediate hostile intention. Unexpected, wild, and violent as they had been, they had given me an irresistible impression of sorrow. The glimpse of the steamboat had for some reason filled those savages with unrestrained grief. The danger, if any, I expounded, was from our proximity to a great human passion let loose. Even extreme grief may ultimately vent itself in violence—but more generally takes the form of apathy . . .

"You should have seen the pilgrims stare! They had no heart to grin, or even to revile me: but I believe they thought me gone mad—with fright, maybe. I delivered a regular lecture. My dear boys, it was no good bothering. Keep a look-out? Well, you may guess I watched the fog for the signs of lifting as a cat watches a mouse; but for anything else our eyes were of no more use to us than if we had been buried miles deep in a heap of cotton-wool. It felt like it, too—choking, warm, stifling. Besides, all I said, though it sounded extravagant, was absolutely true to fact. What we afterwards alluded to as an attack was really an attempt at repulse. The action was very far from being aggressive—it was not even defensive, in the usual sense: it was undertaken under the stress of desperation, and in its essence was purely protective.

"It developed itself, I should say, two hours after the fog lifted, and its commencement was at a spot, roughly speaking, about a mile and a half below Kurtz's station. We had just floundered and flopped round a bend, when I saw an islet, a mere grassy hummock of bright green, in the middle of the stream. It was the only thing of the kind; but as we opened the reach more, I perceived it was the head of a long sandbank, or rather of a chain of shallow patches stretching down the middle of the river. They were discoloured, just awash, and the whole lot was seen just under the water, exactly as a man's backbone is seen running down the middle of his back under the skin. Now, as far as I did see, I could go to the right or to the left of this. I didn't know either channel, of course. The banks looked pretty well alike, the depth appeared the same; but as I had been informed the station was on the west side, I naturally headed for the western passage.

"No sooner had we fairly entered it than I became aware it was much narrower than I had supposed. To the left of us there was the long uninterrupted shoal, and to the right a high, steep bank heavily overgrown with bushes. Above the bush the trees stood in serried ranks. The twigs overhung the current thickly, and from distance to distance a large limb of some tree projected rigidly over the stream. It was then well on in the afternoon, the face of the forest was gloomy, and a broad strip of shadow had already fallen on the water. In this shadow we steamed up—very slowly, as you may imagine. I steered her well inshore—the water being deepest near the bank, as the sounding-pole informed me.

"One of my hungry and forbearing friends was sounding in the bows just below me. This steamboat was exactly like a decked scow. On the deck, there were two little teak-wood houses, with doors and windows. The boiler was in the fore-end, and the machinery right astern. Over the whole there was a light roof, supported on stanchions. The funnel projected through that roof, and in front of the funnel a small cabin built of light planks served for a pilot-house. It contained a couch, two camp-stools, a loaded Martini-Henry leaning in one corner, a tiny table, and the steering-wheel. It had a wide door in front and a broad shutter at each side. All these were always thrown open, of course. I spent my days perched up there on the extreme fore-end of that roof, before the door. At night I slept, or tried to, on the couch. An athletic black belonging to some coast tribe, and educated by my poor predecessor, was the helmsman. He sported a pair of brass earrings, wore a blue cloth wrapper from the waist to the ankles, and thought all the world of himself. He was the most unstable kind of fool I had ever seen. He steered with no end of a swagger while you were by; but if he lost sight of you, he became instantly the prey of an abject funk, and would let that cripple of a steamboat get the upper hand of him in a minute.

"I was looking down at the sounding-pole, and feeling much annoyed to see at each try a little more of it stick out of that river, when I saw my poleman give up the business suddenly, and stretch himself flat on the deck, without even taking the trouble to haul his pole in. He kept hold on it though, and it trailed in the water. At the same time the fireman, whom I could also see below me, sat down abruptly before his furnace and ducked his head. I was amazed. Then I had to look at the river mighty quick, because there was a snag in the fairway. Sticks, little sticks, were flying about—thick: they were whizzing before my nose, dropping below me, striking behind me against my pilot-house. All this time the river, the shore, the woods, were very quiet—perfectly quiet. I could only hear the heavy splashing thump of the stern-wheel and the patter of these things. We cleared the snag clumsily. Arrows, by Jove! We were being shot at! I stepped in quickly to close the shutter on the land-side. That fool-helmsman, his hands on the spokes, was lifting his knees high, stamping his feet, champing his mouth, like a reined-in horse. Confound him! And we were staggering within ten feet of the bank. I had to lean right out to swing the heavy shutter, and I saw a face amongst the leaves on the level with my own, looking at me very fierce and steady and then suddenly, as though a veil had been removed from my eyes, I made out, deep in the tangled gloom, naked breasts, arms, legs, glaring eyes,—the bush was swarming with human limbs in movement, glistening, of bronze colour. The twigs shook, swayed, and rustled, the arrows flew out of them, and then the shutter came to. 'Steer her straight,' I said to the helmsman. He held his head rigid, face forward; but his eyes rolled, he kept on, lifting and setting down his feet gently, his mouth foamed a little. 'Keep quiet!' I said in a fury. I might just as well have ordered a tree not to sway in the wind. I darted out. Below me there was a great scuffle of feet on the iron deck; confused exclamations; a voice screamed, 'Can you turn back?' I caught sight of a V-shaped ripple on the water ahead. What? Another snag! A fusillade burst out under my feet. The pilgrims had opened with their Winchesters, and were simply squirting lead into that bush. A deuce of a lot of smoke came up and drove slowly forward. I swore at it. Now I couldn't see the ripple or the snag either. I stood in the doorway, peering, and the arrows came in swarms. They might have been poisoned, but they looked as though they wouldn't kill a cat. The bush began to howl. Our wood-cutters raised a warlike whoop; the report of a rifle just at my back deafened me. I glanced over my shoulder, and the pilot-house was yet full of noise and smoke when I made a dash at the wheel. The fool-nigger had dropped everything, to throw the shutter open and let off that Martini-Henry. He stood before the wide opening, glaring, and I yelled at him to come back, while I straightened the sudden twist out of that steamboat. There was no room to turn even if I had wanted to, the snag was some-where very near ahead in that confounded smoke, there was no time to lose, so I just crowded her into the bank—right into the bank, where I knew the water was deep.

"We tore slowly along the overhanging bushes in a whirl of bro-ken twigs and flying leaves. The fusillade below stopped short, as I had foreseen it would when the squirts got empty. I threw my head back to a glinting whizz that traversed the pilot-house, in at one shutter-hole and out at the other. Looking past that mad helmsman, who was shaking the empty rifle and yelling at the shore, I saw vague forms of men running bent double, leaping, gliding, indis-tinct, incomplete, evanescent. Something big appeared in the air before the shutter, the rifle went overboard, and the man stepped back swiftly, looked at me over his shoulder in an extraordinary, profound, familiar manner, and fell upon my feet. The side of his head hit the wheel twice, and the end of what appeared to be a long cane clattered round and knocked over a little camp-stool. It looked as though after wrenching that thing from somebody ashore he had lost his balance in the effort. The thin smoke had blown away, we were clear of the snag, and looking ahead I could see that in another hundred yards or so I would be free to sheer off, away from the bank; but my feet felt so very warm and wet that I had to look down. The man had rolled on his back and stared straight up at me; both his hands clutched that cane. It was the shaft of a spear that, either thrown or lunged through the opening, had caught him in the side just below the ribs; the blade had gone in out of sight, after making a frightful gash; my shoes were full; a pool of blood lay very still, gleaming dark-red under the wheel; his eyes shone with an amazing lustre. The fusillade burst out again. He looked at me anxiously, gripping the spear like something precious, with an air of being afraid I would try to take it away from him. I had to make an effort to free my eyes from his gaze and attend to the steering. With one hand I felt above my head for the line of the steam-whistle, and jerked out screech after screech hurriedly. The tumult of angry and warlike yells was checked instantly, and then from the depths of the woods went out such a tremulous and prolonged wail of mournful fear and utter despair as may be imagined to follow the flight of the last hope from the earth. There was a great commotion in the bush; the shower of arrows stopped, a few dropping shots rang out sharply—then silence, in which the languid beat of the stern-wheel came plainly to my ears. I put the helm hard a-starboard at the moment when the pilgrim in pink pyjamas, very hot and agitated, appeared in the doorway. 'The manager sends me—' he began in an official tone, and stopped short. 'Good God!' he said, glaring at the wounded man.

"We two whites stood over him, and his lustrous and inquiring glance enveloped us both. I declare it looked as though he would presently put to us some question in an understandable language; but he died without uttering a sound, without moving a limb, without twitching a muscle. Only in the very last moment, as though in response to some sign we could not see, to some whisper we could not hear, he frowned heavily, and that frown gave to his black death-mask an inconceivably sombre, brooding, and menacing expression. The lustre of the inquiring glance faded swiftly into vacant glassiness. 'Can you steer?' I asked the agent eagerly. He looked very dubious; but I made a grab at his arm, and he understood at once I meant him to steer whether or no. To tell you the truth, I was morbidly anxious to change my shoes and socks. 'He is dead,' murmured the fellow, immensely impressed. 'No doubt about it,' said I, tugging like mad at the shoe-laces. 'And by the way, I suppose Mr. Kurtz is dead as well by this time.'

"For the moment that was the dominant thought. There was a sense of extreme disappointment, as though I had found out I had been striving after something altogether without a substance. I couldn't have been more disgusted if I had travelled all this way for the sole purpose of talking with Mr. Kurtz. Talking with . . . I flung one shoe overboard, and became aware that that was exactly what I had been looking forward to—a talk with Kurtz. I made the strange discovery that I had never imagined him as doing, you know, but as discoursing. I didn't say to myself, 'Now I will never see him,' or 'Now I will never shake him by the hand,' but, 'Now I will never hear him.' The man presented himself as a voice. Not of course that I did not connect him with some sort of action. Hadn't I been told in all the tones of jealousy and admiration that he had collected, bartered, swindled, or stolen more ivory than all the other agents together? That was not the point. The point was in his being a gifted creature, and that of all his gifts the one that stood out pre-eminently, that carried with it a sense of real presence, was his ability to talk, his words—the gift of expression, the bewildering, the illuminating, the most exalted and the most contemptible, the pulsating stream of light, or the deceitful flow from the heart of an impenetrable darkness.

"The other shoe went flying unto the devil-god of that river. I thought, By Jove! it's all over. We are too late; he has vanished—the gift has vanished, by means of some spear, arrow, or club. I will never hear that chap speak after all,—and my sorrow had a startling extravagance of emotion, even such as I had noticed in the howling sorrow of these savages in the bush. I couldn't have felt more of lonely desolation somehow, had I been robbed of a belief or had missed my destiny in life . . . Why do you sigh in this beastly way, somebody? Absurd? Well, absurd. Good Lord! mustn't a man ever— Here, give me some tobacco." . . .

There was a pause of profound stillness, then a match flared, and Marlow's lean face appeared, worn, hollow, with downward folds and dropped eyelids, with an aspect of concentrated attention; and as he took vigorous draws at his pipe, it seemed to retreat and advance out of the night in the regular flicker of the tiny flame. The match went out.

"Absurd!" he cried. "This is the worst of trying to tell . . . Here you all are, each moored with two good addresses, like a hulk with two anchors, a butcher round one corner, a policeman round another, excellent appetites, and temperature normal—you hear—normal from year's end to year's end. And you say, Absurd! Absurd be—exploded! Absurd! My dear boys, what can you expect from a man who out of sheer nervousness had just flung overboard a pair of new shoes! Now I think of it, it is amazing I did not shed tears. I am, upon the whole, proud of my fortitude. I was cut to the quick at the idea of having lost the inestimable privilege of listening to the gifted Kurtz. Of course I was wrong. The privilege was waiting for me. Oh, yes, I heard more than enough. And I was right too. A voice. He was very little more than a voice. And I heard—him—it—this voice—other voices—all of them were so little more than voices—and the memory of that time itself lingers around me, impalpable, like a dying vibration of one immense jabber, silly, atrocious, sordid, savage, or simply mean, without any kind of sense. Voices, voices—even the girl herself—now—"

He was silent for a long time.

"I laid the ghost of his gifts at last with a lie," he began, suddenly. "Girl! What? Did I mention a girl? Oh, she is out of it—completely. They—the women I mean—are out of it—should be out of it. We must help them to stay in that beautiful world of their own, lest ours gets worse. Oh, she had to be out of it. You should have heard the disinterred body of Mr. Kurtz saying, 'My Intended.' You would have perceived directly then how completely she was out of it. And the lofty frontal bone of Mr. Kurtz! They say the hair goes on growing sometimes, but this—ah—specimen, was impressively bald. The wilderness had patted him on the head, and, behold, it was like a ball—an ivory ball; it had caressed him, and—lo!—he had withered; it had taken him, loved him, embraced him, got into his veins, consumed his flesh, and sealed his soul to its own by the inconceivable ceremonies of some devilish initiation. He was its spoiled and pampered favourite. Ivory? I should think so. Heaps of it, stacks of it. The old mud shanty was bursting with it. You would think there was not a single tusk left either above or below the ground in the whole country. 'Mostly fossil,' the manager had remarked, disparagingly. It was no more fossil than I am; but they call it fossil when it is dug up. It appears these niggers do bury the tusks sometimes—but evidently they couldn't bury this parcel deep enough to save the gifted Mr. Kurtz from his fate. We filled the steamboat with it, and had to pile a lot on the deck. Thus he could see and enjoy as long as he could see, because the appreciation of this favour had remained with him to the last. You should have heard him say, 'My ivory.' Oh yes, I heard him. 'My Intended, my ivory, my station, my river, my—' everything belonged to him. It made me hold my breath in expectation of hearing the wilderness burst into a prodigious peal of laughter that would shake the fixed stars in their places. Everything belonged to him—but that was a trifle. The thing was to know what he belonged to, how many powers of darkness claimed him for their own. That was the reflection that made you creepy all over. It was impossible—it was not good for one either—trying to imagine. He had taken a high seat amongst the devils of the land—I mean literally. You can't understand. How could you?—with solid pavement under your feet, surrounded by kind neighbours ready to cheer you or to fall on you, stepping delicately between the butcher and the policeman, in the holy terror of scandal and gallows and lunatic asylums—how can you imagine what particular region of the first ages a man's untrammelled feet may take him into by the way of solitude—utter solitude without a policeman—by the way of silence—utter silence, where no warning voice of a kind neighbour can be heard whispering of public opinion? These little things make all the great difference. When they are gone you must fall back upon your own innate strength, upon your own capacity for faithfulness. Of course you may be too much of a fool to go wrong—too dull even to know you are being assaulted by the powers of darkness. I take it, no fool ever made a bargain for his soul with the devil: the fool is too much of a fool, or the devil too much of a devil—I don't know which. Or you may be such a thunderingly exalted creature as to be altogether deaf and blind to anything but heavenly sights and sounds. Then the earth for you is only a standing place—and whether to be like this is your loss or your gain I won't pretend to say. But most of us are neither one nor the other. The earth for us is a place to live in, where we must put up with sights, with sounds, with smells, too, by Jove!—breathe dead hippo, so to speak, and not be contaminated. And there, don't you see? your strength comes in, the faith in your ability for the digging of unostentatious holes to bury the stuff in—your power of devotion, not to yourself, but to an obscure, back-breaking business. And that's difficult enough. Mind, I am not trying to excuse or even explain—I am trying to account to myself for—for—Mr. Kurtz—for the shade of Mr. Kurtz. This initiated wraith from the back of Nowhere honoured me with its amazing confidence before it vanished altogether. This was because it could speak English to me. The original Kurtz had been educated partly in England, and—as he was good enough to say himself—his sympathies were in the right place. His mother was half-English, his father was half-French. All Europe contributed to the making of Kurtz; and by-and-by I learned that, most appropriately, the International Society for the Suppression of Savage Customs had entrusted him with the making of a report, for its future guidance. And he had written it, too. I've seen it. I've read it. It was eloquent, vibrating with eloquence, but too high-strung, I think. Seventeen pages of close writing he had found time for! But this must have been before his—let us say—nerves, went wrong, and caused him to preside at certain midnight dances ending with unspeakable rites, which—as far as I reluctantly gathered from what I heard at various times—were offered up to him—do you understand?—to Mr. Kurtz himself. But it was a beautiful piece of writing. The opening paragraph, however, in the light of later information, strikes me now as ominous. He began with the argument that we whites, from the point of development we had arrived at, 'must necessarily appear to them [savages] in the nature of supernatural beings—we approach them with the might as of a deity,' and so on, and so on. 'By the simple exercise of our will we can exert a power for good practically unbounded,' etc., etc. From that point he soared and took me with him. The peroration was magnificent, though difficult to remember, you know. It gave me the notion of an exotic Immensity ruled by an august Benevolence. It made me tingle with enthusiasm. This was the unbounded power of eloquence—of words—of burning noble words. There were no practical hints to interrupt the magic current of phrases, unless a kind of note at the foot of the last page, scrawled evidently much later, in an unsteady hand, may be regarded as the exposition of a method. It was very simple, and at the end of that moving appeal to every altruistic sentiment it blazed at you, luminous and terrifying, like a flash of lightning in a serene sky: 'Exterminate all the brutes!' The curious part was that he had apparently forgotten all about that valuable postscriptum, because, later on, when he in a sense came to himself, he repeatedly entreated me to take good care of 'my pamphlet' (he called it), as it was sure to have in the future a good influence upon his career. I had full information about all these things, and, besides, as it turned out, I was to have the care of his memory. I've done enough for it to give me the indisputable right to lay it, if I choose, for an everlasting rest in the dust-bin of progress, amongst all the sweepings and, figuratively speaking, all the dead cats of civilization. But then, you see, I can't choose. He won't be forgotten. Whatever he was, he was not common. He had the power to charm or frighten rudimentary souls into an aggravated witch-dance in his honour; he could also fill the small souls of the pilgrims with bitter misgivings: he had one devoted friend at least, and he had conquered one soul in the world that was neither rudimentary nor tainted with self-seeking. No; I can't forget him, though I am not prepared to affirm the fellow was exactly worth the life we lost in getting to him. I missed my late helmsman awfully,—I missed him even while his body was still lying in the pilot-house. Perhaps you will think it passing strange, this regret for a savage who was of no more account than a grain of sand in a black Sahara. Well, don't you see, he had done something, he had steered; for months I had him at my back—a help—an instrument. It was a kind of partnership. He steered for me—I had to look after him, I worried about his deficiencies, and thus a subtle bond had been created, of which I only became aware when it was suddenly broken. And the intimate profundity of that look he gave me when he received his hurt remains to this day in my memory—like a claim of distant kinship affirmed in a supreme moment.

"Poor fool! If he had only left that shutter alone. He had no restraint, no restraint—just like Kurtz—a tree swayed by the wind. As soon as I had put on a dry pair of slippers, I dragged him out, after first jerking the spear out of his side, which operation I confess I performed with my eyes shut tight. His heels leaped together over the little doorstep; his shoulders were pressed to my breast; I hugged him from behind desperately. Oh! he was heavy, heavy; heavier than any man on earth, I should imagine. Then without more ado I tipped him overboard. The current snatched him as though he had been a wisp of grass, and I saw the body roll over twice before I lost sight of it for ever. All the pilgrims and the manager were then congregated on the awning-deck about the pilot-house, chattering at each other like a flock of excited magpies, and there was a scandalized murmur at my heartless promptitude. What they wanted to keep that body hanging about for I can't guess. Embalm it, maybe. But I had also heard another, and a very ominous, murmur on the deck below. My friends the wood-cutters were likewise scandalized, and with a better show of reason—though I admit that the reason itself was quite inadmissible. Oh, quite! I had made up my mind that if my late helmsman was to be eaten, the fishes alone should have him. He had been a very second-rate helmsman while alive, but now he was dead he might have become a first-class temptation, and possibly cause some startling trouble. Besides, I was anxious to take the wheel, the man in pink pyjamas showing himself a hopeless duffer at the business.

"This I did directly the simple funeral was over. We were going half-speed, keeping right in the middle of the stream, and I listened to the talk about me. They had given up Kurtz, they had given up the station; Kurtz was dead, and the station had been burnt—and so on—and so on. The red-haired pilgrim was beside himself with the thought that at least this poor Kurtz had been properly avenged.'Say! We must have made a glorious slaughter of them in the bush. Eh? What do you think? Say?' He positively danced, the bloodthirsty little gingery beggar. And he had nearly fainted when he saw the wounded man! I could not help saying, 'You made a glorious lot of smoke, anyhow.' I had seen, from the way the tops of the bushes rustled and flew, that almost all the shots

CANNABALISM !

had gone too high. You can't hit anything unless you take aim and fire from the shoulder; but these chaps fired from the hip with their eyes shut. The retreat, I maintained—and I was right—was caused by the screeching of the steam-whistle. Upon this they forgot Kurtz, and began to howl at me with indignant protests.

"The manager stood by the wheel murmuring confidentially about the necessity of getting well away down the river before dark at all events, when I saw in the distance a clearing on the river-side and the outlines of some sort of building. 'What's this?' I asked. He clapped his hands in wonder. 'The station!' he cried. I edged in at once, still going half-speed.

"Through my glasses I saw the slope of a hill interspersed with rare trees and perfectly free from undergrowth. A long decaying building on the summit was half buried in the high grass; the large holes in the peaked roof gaped black from afar; the jungle and the woods made a background. There was no enclosure or fence of any kind; but there had been one apparently, for near the house half-a-dozen slim posts remained in a row, roughly trimmed, and with their upper ends ornamented with round carved balls. The rails, or what-ever there had been between, had disappeared. Of course the forest surrounded all that. The river-bank was clear, and on the water-side I saw a white man under a hat like a cartwheel beckoning persis-tently with his whole arm. Examining the edge of the forest above and below, I was almost certain I could see movements—human forms gliding here and there. I steamed past prudently, then stopped the engines and let her drift down. The man on the shore began to shout, urging us to land. 'We have been attacked,' screamed the manager. 'I know—I know. It's all right,' yelled back the other, as cheerful as you please. 'Come along. It's all right. I am glad.'

"His aspect reminded me of something I had seen—something funny I had seen somewhere. As I manoeuvred to get alongside, I was asking myself, 'What does this fellow look like?' Suddenly I got it. He looked like a harlequin. His clothes had been made of some stuff that was brown holland probably, but it was covered with patches all over, with bright patches, blue, red, and yellow,—

patches on the back, patches on the front, patches on elbows, on knees; coloured binding around his jacket, scarlet edging at the bottom of his trousers; and the sunshine made him look extremely gay and wonderfully neat withal, because you could see how beautifully all this patching had been done. A beardless, boyish face, very fair, no feature to speak of, nose peeling, little blue eyes, smiles and frowns chasing each other over that open countenance like sunshine and shadow on a wind-swept plain. 'Look out, captain!' he cried; 'there's a snag lodged in here last night.' What! Another snag? I confess I swore shamefully. I had nearly holed my cripple, to finish off that charming trip. The harlequin on the bank turned his little pug-nose up to me. 'You English?' he asked, all smiles. 'Are you?' I shouted from the wheel. The smiles vanished, and he shook his head as if sorry for my disappointment. Then he brightened up. 'Never mind!' he cried, encouragingly. 'Are we in time?' I asked. 'He is up there,' he replied, with a toss of the head up the hill, and becoming gloomy all of a sudden. His face was like the autumn sky, overcast one moment and bright the next.

"When the manager, escorted by the pilgrims, all of them armed to the teeth, had gone to the house this chap came on board. 'I say, I don't like this. These natives are in the bush,' I said. He assured me earnestly it was all right. 'They are simple people,' he added; 'well, I am glad you came. It took me all my time to keep them off.' 'But you said it was all right,' I cried. 'Oh, they meant no harm,' he said; and as I stared he corrected himself, 'Not exactly.' Then vivaciously, 'My faith, your pilot-house wants a clean-up!' In the next breath he advised me to keep enough steam on the boiler to blow the whistle in case of any trouble. 'One good screech will do more for you than all your rifles. They are simple people,' he repeated. He rattled away at such a rate he quite overwhelmed me. He seemed to be trying to make up for lots of silence, and actually hinted, laughing, that such was the case. 'Don't you talk with Mr. Kurtz?' I said. 'You don't talk with that man—you listen to him,' he exclaimed with severe exaltation. 'But now—' He waved his arm, and in the twinkling of an eye was in the uttermost depths of despondency. In a moment he came up again with a jump, possessed himself of both hands, shook them continuously, while he gabbled: 'Brother sailor . . . honour . . . pleasure . . . delight . . . introduce myself . . . Russian . . . son of an arch-priest . . . Government of Tambov . . . What? Tobacco! English tobacco; the excellent English tobacco! Now, that's brotherly. Smoke? Where's a sailor that does not smoke?'

'The pipe soothed him, and gradually I made out he had run away from school, had gone to sea in a Russian ship; ran away again; served some time in English ships; was now reconciled with the arch-priest. He made a point of that. 'But when one is young one must see things, gather experience, ideas; enlarge the mind.' 'Here!' I interrupted. 'You can never tell! Here I met Mr. Kurtz,' he said, youthfully solemn and reproachful. I held my tongue after that. It appears he had persuaded a Dutch trading-house on the coast to fit him out with stores and goods, and had started for the interior with a light heart, and no more idea of what would happen to him than a baby. He had been wandering about that river for nearly two years alone, cut off from everybody and everything. 'I am not so young as I look. I am twenty-five,' he said. 'At first old Van Shuyten would tell me to go to the devil,' he narrated with keen enjoyment; 'but I stuck to him, and talked and talked, till at last he got afraid I would talk the hind-leg off his favourite dog, so he gave me some cheap things and a few guns, and told me he hoped he would never see my face again. Good old Dutchman. Van Shuyten. I've sent him one small lot of ivory a year ago, so that he can't call me a little thief when I get back. I hope he got it. And for the rest I don't care. I had some wood stacked for you. That was my old house. Did you see?'

"I gave him Towson's book. He made as though he would kiss me, but restrained himself. 'The only book I had left, and I thought I had lost it,' he said, looking at it ecstatically. 'So many accidents happen to a man going about alone, you know. Canoes get upset sometimes—and sometimes you've got to clear out so quickly when the people get angry.' He thumbed the pages. 'You made notes in Russian?' I asked. He nodded. 'I thought they were written in cipher,' I said. He laughed, then became serious. 'I had lots of trouble to keep these people off,' he said. 'Did they want to kill you?' I asked.

'Oh, no!' he cried, and checked himself. 'Why did they attack us?' I pursued. He hesitated, then said shamefacedly, 'They don't want him to go.' 'Don't they?' I said, curiously. He nodded a nod full of mystery and wisdom. 'I tell you,' he cried, 'this man has enlarged my mind.' He opened his arms wide, staring at me with his little blue eyes that were perfectly round."

III

"I looked at him, lost in astonishment. There he was before me, in motley, as though he had absconded from a troupe of mimes, enthusiastic, fabulous. His very existence was improbable, inexplicable, and altogether bewildering. He was an insoluble problem. It was inconceivable how he had existed, how he had succeeded in getting so far, how he had managed to remain—why he did not instantly disappear. 'I went a little farther,' he said, 'then still a little farther—till I had gone so far that I don't know how I'll ever get back. Never mind. Plenty time. I can manage. You take Kurtz away quick—quick—I tell you.' The glamour of youth enveloped his parti-coloured rags, his destitution, his loneliness, the essential desolation of his futile wanderings. For months—for years—his life hadn't been worth a day's purchase: and there he was gallantly, thoughtlessly alive, to all appearance indestructible solely by the virtue of his few years and of his unreflecting audacity. I was seduced into something like admiration—like envy. Glamour urged him on, glamour kept him unscathed. He surely wanted nothing from the wilderness but space to breathe in and to push on through. His need was to exist, and to move onwards at the greatest possible risk, and with a maximum of privation. If the absolutely pure, uncalculating, unpractical spirit of adventure had ever ruled a human being, it ruled this be-patched youth. I almost envied him the possession of this modest and clear flame. It seemed to have consumed all thought of self so completely, that even while he was talking to you, you forgot that it was he—the man before your eyes—who had gone through these things. I did not envy him his devotion to Kurtz, though. He had not meditated over it. It came to him, and he accepted it with a sort of eager fatalism. I must say that to me it appeared about the most dangerous thing in every way he had come upon so far.

"They had come together unavoidably, like two ships becalmed near each other, and lay rubbing sides at last. I suppose Kurtz wanted an audience, because on a certain occasion, when encamped in the forest, they had talked all night, or more probably Kurtz had talked. 'We talked of everything,' he said, quite transported at the recollection. 'I forgot there was such a thing as sleep. The night did not seem to last an hour. Everything! Everything! . . . Of love, too.' 'Ah, he talked to you of love?' I said, much amused. 'It isn't what you think,' he cried, almost passionately. 'It was in general. He made me see things—things.'

"He threw his arms up. We were on deck at the time, and the headman of my wood-cutters, lounging near by, turned upon him his heavy and glittering eyes. I looked around, and I don't know why, but I assure you that never, never before, did this land, this river, this jungle, the very arch of this blazing sky, appear to me so hopeless and so dark, so impenetrable to human thought, so pitiless to human weakness. 'And, ever since, you have been with him, of course?' I said.

"On the contrary. It appears their intercourse had been very much broken by various causes. He had, as he informed me proudly, managed to nurse Kurtz through two illnesses (he alluded to it as you would to some risky feat), but as a rule Kurtz wandered alone, far in the depths of the forest. 'Very often coming to this station, I had to wait days and days before he would turn up,' he said. 'Ah, it was worth waiting for!—sometimes.' 'What was he doing? exploring or what?' I asked. 'Oh, yes, of course'; he had discovered lots of villages, a lake, too—he did not know exactly in what direction; it was dangerous to inquire too much—but mostly his expeditions had been for ivory. 'But he had no goods to trade with by that time,' I objected. 'There's a good lot of cartridges left even yet,' he answered, looking away. 'To speak plainly, he raided the country,' I said. He nodded. 'Not alone, surely!' He muttered something about the villages round that lake. 'Kurtz got the tribe to follow him, did he?' I suggested. He fidgeted a little. 'They adored him,' he said. The tone of these words was so extraordinary that I looked at him searchingly. It was curious to see his mingled eagerness and reluctance to speak of Kurtz. The man filled his life, occupied his thoughts, swayed his emotions. 'What can you expect?' he burst out; 'he came to them with thunder and lightning, you know—and they had never seen anything like it—and very terrible. He could be very terrible. You can't judge Mr. Kurtz as you would an ordinary man. No, no, no! Now—just to give you an idea—I don't mind telling you, he wanted to shoot me, too, one day—but I don't judge him.' 'Shoot you!' I cried. 'What for?' 'Well, I had a small lot of ivory the chief of that village near my house gave me. You see I used to shoot game for them. Well, he wanted it, and wouldn't hear reason. He declared he would shoot me unless I gave him the ivory and then cleared out of the country, because he could do so, and had a fancy for it, and there was nothing on earth to prevent him killing whom he jolly well pleased. And it was true, too. I gave him the ivory. What did I care! But I didn't clear out. No, no. I couldn't leave him. I had to be careful, of course, till we got friendly again for a time. He had his second illness then. Afterwards I had to keep out of the way; but I didn't mind. He was living for the most part in those villages on the lake. When he came down to the river, sometimes he would take to me, and sometimes it was better for me to be careful. This man suffered too much. He hated all this, and somehow he couldn't get away. When I had a chance I begged him to try and leave while there was time; I offered to go back with him. And he would say yes, and then he would remain; go off on another ivory hunt; disappear for weeks; forget himself amongst these people—forget himself— you know.' 'Why! he's mad,' I said. He protested indignantly. Mr.

Kurtz couldn't be mad. If I had heard him talk, only two days ago, I wouldn't dare hint at such a thing . . . I had taken up my binoculars while we talked, and was looking at the shore, sweeping the limit of the forest at each side and at the back of the house. The consciousness of there being people in that bush, so silent, so quiet—as silent and quiet as the ruined house on the hill—made me uneasy. There was no sign on the face of nature of this amazing tale that was not so much told as suggested to me in desolate exclamations, completed by shrugs, in interrupted phrases, in hints ending in deep sighs. The woods were unmoved, like a mask—heavy, like the closed door of a prison—they looked with their air of hidden knowledge, of patient expectation, of unapproachable silence. The Russian was explaining to me that it was only lately that Mr. Kurtz had come down to the river, bringing along with him all the fighting men of that lake tribe. He had been absent for several months—getting himself adored, I suppose—and had come down unexpectedly, with the intention to all appearance of making a raid either across the river or down stream. Evidently the appetite for more ivory had got the better of the—what shall I say?—less material aspirations. However he had got much worse suddenly. 'I heard he was lying helpless, and so I came up—took my chance,' said the Russian. 'Oh, he is bad, very bad.' I directed my glass to the house. There were no signs of life, but there was the ruined roof, the long mud wall peeping above the grass, with three little square window-holes, no two the same size: all this brought within reach of my hand, as it were. And then I made a brusque movement, and one of the remaining posts of that vanished fence leaped up in the field of my glass. You remember I told you I had been struck at the distance by certain attempts at ornamentation, rather remarkable in the ruinous aspect of the place. Now I had suddenly a nearer view, and its first result was to make me throw my head back as if before a blow. Then I went carefully from post to post with my glass, and I saw my mistake. These round knobs were not ornamental but symbolic; they were expressive and puzzling, striking and disturbing—food for thought and also for the vultures if there had been any looking down from the sky; but at all events for such ants as were industrious enough to ascend the pole.

They would have been even more impressive, those heads on the stakes, if their faces had not been turned to the house. Only one, the first I had made out, was facing my way. I was not so shocked as you may think. The start back I had given was really nothing but a movement of surprise. I had expected to see a knob of wood there, you know. I returned deliberately to the first I had seen—and there it was, black, dried, sunken, with closed eyelids—a head that seemed to sleep at the top of that pole, and, with the shrunken dry lips showing a narrow white line of teeth, was smiling, too, smiling continuously at some endless and jocose dream of that eternal slumber.

"I am not disclosing any trade secrets. In fact, the manager said afterwards that Mr. Kurtz's methods had ruined the district. I have no opinion on that point, but I want you clearly to understand that there was nothing exactly profitable in these heads being there. They only showed that Mr. Kurtz lacked restraint in the gratification of his various lusts, that there was something wanting in him— some small matter which, when the pressing need arose, could not be found under his magnificent eloquence. Whether he knew of this deficiency himself I can't say. I think the knowledge came to him at last—only at the very last. But the wilderness had found him out early, and had taken on him a terrible vengeance for the fantastic invasion. I think it had whispered to him things about himself which he did not know, things of which he had no conception till he took counsel with this great solitude—and the whisper had proved irresistibly fascinating. It echoed loudly within him because he was hollow at the core . . . I put down the glass, and the head that had appeared near enough to be spoken to seemed at once to have leaped away from me into inaccessible distance.

"The admirer of Mr. Kurtz was a bit crestfallen. In a hurried, indistinct voice he began to assure me he had not dared to take these—say, symbols—down. He was not afraid of the natives; they would not stir till Mr. Kurtz gave the word. His ascendancy was extraordinary. The camps of these people surrounded the place, and the chiefs came every day to see him. They would crawl . . . 'I don't want to know anything of the ceremonies used when approaching Mr. Kurtz,' I shouted. Curious, this feeling that came over me that such details would be more intolerable than those heads drying on the stakes under Mr. Kurtz's windows. After all, that was only a savage sight, while I seemed at one bound to have been transported into some lightless region of subtle horrors, where pure, uncomplicated savagery was a positive relief, being something that had a right to exist—obviously—in the sunshine. The young man looked at me with surprise. I suppose it did not occur to him that Mr. Kurtz was no idol of mine. He forgot I hadn't heard any of these splendid monologues on, what was it? on love, justice, conduct of life—or what not. If it had come to crawling before Mr. Kurtz, he crawled as much as the veriest savage of them all. I had no idea of the conditions, he said: these heads were the heads of rebels. I shocked him excessively by laughing. Rebels! What would be the next definition I was to hear? There had been enemies, criminals, workers—and these were rebels. Those rebellious heads looked very subdued to me on their sticks. 'You don't know how such a life tries a man like Kurtz,' cried Kurtz's last disciple. 'Well, and you?' I said. 'I! I! I am a simple man. I have no great thoughts. I want nothing from anybody. How can you compare me to? . . .' His feelings were too much for speech, and suddenly he broke down. 'I don't understand,' he groaned. 'I've been doing my best to keep him alive, and that's enough. I had no hand in all this. I have no abilities. There hasn't been a drop of medicine or a mouthful of invalid food for months here. He was shamefully abandoned. A man like this, with such ideas. Shamefully! Shamefully! I—I—haven't slept for the last ten nights . . .'

"His voice lost itself in the calm of the evening. The long shadows of the forest had slipped down hill while we talked, had gone far beyond the ruined hovel, beyond the symbolic row of stakes. All this was in the gloom, while we down there were yet in the sunshine, and the stretch of the river abreast of the clearing glittered in a still and dazzling splendour, with a murky and overshadowed bend above and below. Not a living soul was seen on the shore. The bushes did not rustle.

"Suddenly round the corner of the house a group of men appeared, as though they had come up from the ground. They waded waist-deep in the grass, in a compact body, bearing an improvised stretcher in their midst. Instantly, in the emptiness of the landscape, a cry arose whose shrillness pierced the still air like a sharp arrow flying straight to the very heart of the land; and, as if by enchantment, streams of human beings—of naked human beings—with spears in their hands, with bows, with shields, with wild glances and savage movements, were poured into the clearing by the dark-faced and pensive forest. The bushes shook, the grass swayed for a time, and then everything stood still in attentive immobility.

" 'Now, if he does not say the right thing to them we are all done for,' said the Russian at my elbow. The knot of men with the stretcher had stopped, too, halfway to the steamer, as if petrified. I saw the man on the stretcher sit up, lank and with an uplifted arm, above the shoulders of the bearers. 'Let us hope that the man who can talk so well of love in general will find some particular reason to spare us this time,' I said. I resented bitterly the absurd danger of our situation, as if to be at the mercy of that atrocious phantom had been a dishonouring necessity. I could not hear a sound, but through my glasses I saw the thin arm extended commandingly, the lower jaw moving, the eyes of that apparition shining darkly far in its bony head that nodded with grotesque jerks. Kurtz—Kurtz— that means short in German—don't it? Well, the name was as true as everything else in his life—and death. He looked at least seven feet long. His covering had fallen off, and his body emerged from it pitiful and appalling as from a winding-sheet. I could see the cage of his ribs all astir, the bones of his arm waving. It was as though an animated image of death carved out of old ivory had been shaking its hand with menaces at a motionless crowd of men made of dark and glittering bronze. I saw him open his mouth wide—it gave him a weirdly voracious aspect, as though he had wanted to swallow all the air, all the earth, all the men before him. A deep voice reached me faintly. He must have been shouting. He fell back suddenly. The stretcher shook as the bearers staggered forward again, and almost at the same time I noticed that the crowd of savages was vanishing without any perceptible movement of retreat, as if the forest that had ejected these beings so suddenly had drawn them in again as the breath is drawn in a long aspiration.

"Some of the pilgrims behind the stretcher carried his arms— two shot-guns, a heavy rifle, and a light revolver-carbine—the thunderbolts of that pitiful Jupiter. The manager bent over him murmuring as he walked beside his head. They laid him down in one of the little cabins—just a room for a bedplace and a camp-stool or two, you know. We had brought his belated correspondence, and a lot of torn envelopes and open letters littered his bed. His hand roamed feebly amongst these papers. I was struck by the fire of his eyes and the composed languor of his expression. It was not so much the exhaustion of disease. He did not seem in pain. This shadow looked satiated and calm, as though for the moment it had had its fill of all the emotions.

"He rustled one of the letters, and looking straight in my face said, 'I am glad.' Somebody had been writing to him about me. These special recommendations were turning up again. The volume of tone he emitted without effort, almost without the trouble of moving his lips, amazed me. A voice! a voice! It was grave, profound, vibrating, while the man did not seem capable of a whisper. However, he had enough strength in him—factitious no doubt—to very nearly make an end of us, as you shall hear directly.

"The manager appeared silently in the doorway; I stepped out at once and he drew the curtain after me. The Russian, eyed curiously by the pilgrims, was staring at the shore. I followed the direction of his glance.

"Dark human shapes could be made out in the distance, flitting indistinctly against the gloomy border of the forest, and near the river two bronze figures, leaning on tall spears, stood in the sunlight under fantastic head-dresses of spotted skins, warlike and still in statuesque repose. And from right to left along the lighted shore moved a wild and gorgeous apparition of a woman.

"She walked with measured steps, draped in striped and fringed cloths, treading the earth proudly, with a slight jingle and flash of barbarous ornaments. She carried her head high; her hair was done in the shape of a helmet; she had brass leggings to the knees, brass wire gauntlets to the elbow, a crimson spot on her tawny cheek, innumerable necklaces of glass beads on her neck; bizarre things, charms, gifts of witch-men, that hung about her, glittered and trembled at every step. She must have had the value of several elephant tusks upon her. She was savage and superb, wild-eyed and magnificent; there was something ominous and stately in her deliberate progress. And in the hush that had fallen suddenly upon the whole sorrowful land, the immense wilderness, the colossal body of the fecund and mysterious life seemed to look at her, pensive, as though it had been looking at the image of its own tenebrous and passionate soul.

"She came abreast of the steamer, stood still, and faced us. Her long shadow fell to the water's edge. Her face had a tragic and fierce aspect of wild sorrow and of dumb pain mingled with the fear of some struggling, half-shaped resolve. She stood looking at us without a stir, and like the wilderness itself, with an air of brooding over an inscrutable purpose. A whole minute passed, and then she made a step forward. There was a low jingle, a glint of yellow metal, a sway of fringed draperies, and she stopped as if her heart had failed her. The young fellow by my side growled. The pilgrims murmured at my back. She looked at us all as if her life had depended upon the unswerving steadiness of her glance. Suddenly she opened her bared arms and threw them up rigid above her head, as though in an uncontrollable desire to touch the sky, and at the same time the swift shadows darted out on the earth, swept around on the river, gathering the steamer into a shadowy embrace. A formidable silence hung over the scene.

"She turned away slowly, walked on, following the bank, and passed into the bushes to the left. Once only her eyes gleamed back at us in the dusk of the thickets before she disappeared.

" 'If she had offered to come aboard I really think I would have tried to shoot her,' said the man of patches, nervously. 'I had been risking my life every day for the last fortnight to keep her out of the house. She got in one day and kicked up a row about those miserable rags I picked up in the storeroom to mend my clothes with. I wasn't decent. At least it must have been that, for she talked like a fury to Kurtz for an hour, pointing at me now and then. I don't understand the dialect of this tribe. Luckily for me, I fancy Kurtz felt too ill that day to care, or there would have been mischief. I don't understand . . . No—it's too much for me. Ah, well, it's all over now.'

"At this moment I heard Kurtz's deep voice behind the curtain: 'Save me!—save the ivory, you mean. Don't tell me. Save *me!* Why, I've had to save you. You are interrupting my plans now. Sick! Sick! Not so sick as you would like to believe. Never mind. I'll carry my ideas out yet—I will return. I'll show you what can be done. You with your little peddling notions—you are interfering with me. I will return. I . . .'

"The manager came out. He did me the honour to take me under the arm and lead me aside. 'He is very low, very low,' he said. He considered it necessary to sigh, but neglected to be consistently sorrowful. 'We have done all we could for him—haven't we? But there is no disguising the fact, Mr. Kurtz has done more harm than good to the Company. He did not see the time was not ripe for vigorous action. Cautiously, cautiously—that's my principle. We must be cautious yet. The district is closed to us for a time. Deplorable! Upon the whole, the trade will suffer. I don't deny there is a remarkable quantity of ivory—mostly fossil. We must save it, at all events—but look how precarious the position is—and why? Because the method is unsound.' 'Do you,' said I, looking at the shore, 'call it "unsound method"?' 'Without doubt,' he exclaimed, hotly. 'Don't you?' . . .

" 'No method at all,' I murmured after a while. 'Exactly,' he exulted. 'I anticipated this. Shows a complete want of judgment. It is my duty to point it out in the proper quarter.' 'Oh,' said I, 'that fellow—what's his name?—the brickmaker, will make a readable report for you.' He appeared confounded for a moment. It seemed to me I had never breathed an atmosphere so vile, and I turned mentally to Kurtz for relief—positively for relief. 'Nevertheless I think Mr. Kurtz is a remarkable man,' I said with emphasis. He started, dropped on me a cold heavy glance, said very quietly 'He *was*,' and turned his back on me. My hour of favour was over; I found myself lumped along with Kurtz as a partisan of methods for which the time was not ripe: I was unsound! Ah! <u>but it was something to have at least a choice of nightmares.</u>

"I had turned to the wilderness really, not to Mr. Kurtz, who, I was ready to admit, was as good as buried. And for a moment it seemed to me as if I also were buried in a vast grave full of unspeakable secrets. I felt an intolerable weight oppressing my breast, the smell of the damp earth, the unseen presence of victorious corruption, the darkness of an impenetrable night . . . The Russian tapped me on the shoulder. I heard him mumbling and stammering something about 'brother seaman—couldn't conceal—knowledge of matters that would affect Mr. Kurtz's reputation.' I waited. For him evidently Mr. Kurtz was not in his grave; I suspect that for him Mr. Kurtz was one of the immortals. 'Well!' said I at last, 'speak out. As it happens, I am Mr. Kurtz's friend—in a way.'

"He stated with a good deal of formality that had we not been 'of the same profession,' he would have kept the matter to himself without regard to consequences. 'He suspected there was an active ill will towards him on the part of these white men that—' 'You are right,' I said, remembering a certain conversation I had overheard. 'The manager thinks you ought to be hanged.' He showed a concern at this intelligence which amused me at first. 'I had better get out of the way quietly,' he said, earnestly. 'I can do no more for Kurtz now, and they would soon find some excuse. What's to stop them? There's a military post three hundred miles from here.' 'Well, upon my word,' said I, 'perhaps you had better go if you have any friends amongst the savages near by.' 'Plenty,' he said. 'They are simple people—and I want nothing, you know.' He stood biting his lip, then: 'I don't want any harm to happen to these whites here, but of course I was thinking of Mr. Kurtz's reputation—but you are a brother seaman and—' 'All right,' said I, after a time. 'Mr. Kurtz's reputation is safe with me.' I did not know how truly I spoke.

"He informed me, lowering his voice, that it was Kurtz who had ordered the attack to be made on the steamer. 'He hated sometimes the idea of being taken away—and then again . . . But I don't understand these matters. I am a simple man. He thought it would scare you away—that you would give it up, thinking him dead. I could not stop him. Oh, I had an awful time of it this last month.' 'Very well,' I said. 'He is all right now.' 'Ye-e-es,' he muttered, not very convinced apparently. 'Thanks,' said I; 'I shall keep my eyes open.' 'But quiet—eh?' he urged, anxiously. 'It would be awful for his reputation if anybody here—' I promised a complete discretion with great gravity. 'I have a canoe and three black fellows waiting not very far. I am off. Could you give me a few Martini-Henry cartridges?' I could, and did, with proper secrecy. He helped himself, with a wink at me, to a handful of my tobacco. 'Between sailors— you know—good English tobacco.' At the door of the pilot-house he turned round—'I say, haven't you a pair of shoes you could spare?' He raised one leg. 'Look.' The soles were tied with knotted strings sandal-wise under his bare feet. I rooted out an old pair, at which he looked with admiration before tucking it under his left arm. One of his pockets (bright red) was bulging with cartridges, from the other (dark blue) peeped 'Towson's Inquiry,' etc., etc. He seemed to think himself excellently well equipped for a renewed encounter with the wilderness. 'Ah! I'll never, never meet such a man again. You ought to have heard him recite poetry—his own, too, it was, he told me. Poetry!' He rolled his eyes at the recollection of these delights. 'Oh, he enlarged my mind!' 'Good-bye,' said I. He shook hands and vanished in the night. Sometimes I ask myself whether I had ever really seen him—whether it was possible to meet such a phenomenon! . . .

"When I woke up shortly after midnight his warning came to my mind with its hint of danger that seemed, in the starred darkness, real enough to make me get up for the purpose of having a look round. On the hill a big fire burned, illuminating fitfully a crooked corner of the station-house. One of the agents with a picket of a few of our blacks, armed for the purpose, was keeping guard over the ivory; but deep within the forest, red gleams that wavered, that seemed to sink and rise from the ground amongst confused columnar shapes of intense blackness, showed the exact position of the camp where Mr. Kurtz's adorers were keeping their uneasy vigil. The monotonous beating of a big drum filled the air with muffled shocks and a lingering vibration. A steady droning sound of many men chanting each to himself some weird incantation came out from the black, flat wall of the woods as the humming of bees comes out of a hive, and had a strange narcotic effect upon my half-awake senses. I believe I dozed off leaning over the rail, till an abrupt burst of yells, an overwhelming outbreak of a pent-up and mysterious frenzy, woke me up in a bewildered wonder. It was cut short all at once, and the low droning went on with an effect of audible and soothing silence. I glanced casually into the little cabin. A light was burning within, but Mr. Kurtz was not there.

"I think I would have raised an outcry if I had believed my eyes. But I didn't believe them at first—the thing seemed so impossible. The fact is I was completely unnerved by a sheer blank fright, pure abstract terror, unconnected with any distinct shape of physical danger. What made this emotion so overpowering was—how shall I define it?—the moral shock I received, as if something altogether monstrous, intolerable to thought and odious to the soul, had been thrust upon me unexpectedly. This lasted of course the merest fraction of a second, and then the usual sense of commonplace, deadly danger, the possibility of a sudden onslaught and massacre, or something of the kind, which I saw impending, was positively welcome and composing. It pacified me, in fact, so much, that I did not raise an alarm.

"There was an agent buttoned up inside an ulster and sleeping on a chair on deck within three feet of me. The yells had not awakened him; he snored very slightly; I left him to his slumbers and leaped ashore. I did not betray Mr. Kurtz—it was ordered I should never betray him—it was written I should be loyal to the nightmare of my choice. I was anxious to deal with this shadow by myself alone,—and to this day I don't know why I was so jealous of sharing with anyone the peculiar blackness of that experience.

"As soon as I got on the bank I saw a trail—a broad trail through the grass. I remember the exultation with which I said to myself, 'He can't walk—he is crawling on all-fours—I've got him.' The grass was wet with dew. I strode rapidly with clenched fists. I fancy I had some vague notion of falling upon him and giving him a drubbing. I don't know. I had some imbecile thoughts. The knitting old woman with the cat obtruded herself upon my memory as a most improper person to be sitting at the other end of such an affair. I saw a row of pilgrims squirting lead in the air out of Winchesters held to the hip. I thought I would never get back to the steamer, and imagined myself living alone and unarmed in the woods to an advanced age. Such silly things—you know. And I remember I confounded the beat of the drum with the beating of my heart, and was pleased at its calm regularity.

"I kept to the track though—then stopped to listen. The night was very clear; a dark blue space, sparkling with dew and starlight, in which black things stood very still. I thought I could see a kind of motion ahead of me. I was strangely cocksure of everything that night. I actually left the track and ran in a wide semicircle (I verily believe chuckling to myself) so as to get in front of that stir, of that motion I had seen—if indeed I had seen anything. I was circumventing Kurtz as though it had been a boyish game.

"I came upon him, and, if he had not heard me coming, I would have fallen over him, too, but he got up in time. He rose, unsteady, long, pale, indistinct, like a vapour exhaled by the earth, and swayed slightly, misty and silent before me; while at my back the fires loomed between the trees, and the murmur of many voices issued from the forest. I had cut him off cleverly; but when actually confronting him I seemed to come to my senses, I saw the danger in its right proportion. It was by no means over yet. Suppose he began to shout? Though he could hardly stand, there was still plenty of vigour in his voice. 'Go away—hide yourself,' he said, in that profound tone. It was very awful. I glanced back. We were within thirty yards from the nearest fire. A black figure stood up, strode on long black legs, waving long black arms, across the glow. It had horns—antelope horns, I think—on its head. Some sorcerer, some witchman, no doubt: it looked fiend-like enough. 'Do you know what you are doing?' I whispered. 'Perfectly,' he answered, raising his voice for that single word: it sounded to me far off and yet loud, like a hail through a speaking-trumpet. If he makes a row we are lost, I thought to myself. This clearly was not a case for fisticuffs, even apart from the very natural aversion I had to beat that Shadow—this wandering and tormented thing. 'You will be lost,' I said—'utterly lost.' One gets sometimes such a flash of inspiration, you know. I did say the right thing, though indeed he could not have been more irretrievably lost than he was at this very moment, when the foundations of our intimacy were being laid—to endure—to endure—even to the end—even beyond.

" 'I had immense plans,' he muttered irresolutely. 'Yes,' said I; 'but if you try to shout I'll smash your head with—' There was not a stick or a stone near. 'I will throttle you for good,' I corrected myself. 'I was on the threshold of great things,' he pleaded, in a voice of longing, with a wistfulness of tone that made my blood run cold. 'And now for this stupid scoundrel—' 'Your success in Europe is assured in any case,' I affirmed, steadily. I did not want to have the throttling of him, you understand—and indeed it would have been very little use for any practical purpose. I tried to break the spell—the heavy, mute spell of the wilderness—that seemed to draw him to its pitiless breast by the awakening of forgotten and brutal instincts, by the memory of gratified and monstrous passions. This alone, I was convinced, had driven him out to the edge of the forest, to the bush, towards the gleam of fires, the throb of drums, the drone of weird incantations; this alone had beguiled his unlawful soul beyond the bounds of permitted aspirations. And, don't you see, the terror of the position was not in being knocked on the head—though I had a very lively sense of that danger, too—but in this, that I had to deal with a being to whom I could not appeal in the name of anything high or low. I had, even like the niggers, to invoke him—himself—his own exalted and incredible degradation. There was nothing either above or below him, and I knew it. He had kicked himself loose of the earth. Confound the man! he had kicked the very earth to pieces. He was alone, and I before him did not know whether I stood on the ground or floated in the air. I've been telling you what we said—repeating the phrases we pronounced—but what's the good? They were common everyday words—the familiar, vague sounds exchanged on every waking day of life. But what of that? They had behind them, to my mind, the terrific suggestiveness of words heard in dreams, of phrases spoken in night-mares. Soul! If anybody had ever struggled with a soul, I am the man. And I wasn't arguing with a lunatic either. Believe me or not, his intelligence was perfectly clear—concentrated, it is true, upon himself with horrible intensity, yet clear; and therein was my only chance—barring, of course, the killing him there and then, which wasn't so good, on account of unavoidable noise. But his soul was mad. Being alone in the wilderness, it had looked within itself, and, by heavens! I tell you, it had gone mad. I had—for my sins, I suppose—to go through the ordeal of looking into it myself. No eloquence could have been so withering to one's belief in mankind as his final burst of sincerity. He struggled with himself, too. I saw it,—I heard it. I saw the inconceivable mystery of a soul that knew no restraint, no faith, and no fear, yet struggling blindly with itself. I kept my head pretty well; but when I had him at last stretched on the couch, I wiped my forehead, while my legs shook under me as though I had carried half a ton on my back down that hill. And yet I had only supported him, his bony arm clasped round my neck—and he was not much heavier than a child.

"When next day we left at noon, the crowd, of whose presence behind the curtain of trees I had been acutely conscious all the time, flowed out of the woods again, filled the clearing, covered the slope with a mass of naked, breathing, quivering, bronze bodies. I steamed up a bit, then swung downstream, and two thousand eyes followed the evolutions of the splashing, thumping, fierce river-demon beating the water with its terrible tail and breathing black smoke into the air. In front of the first rank, along the river, three men, plastered with bright red earth from head to foot, strutted to and fro restlessly. When we came abreast again, they faced the river, stamped their feet, nodded their horned heads, swayed their scarlet bodies; they shook towards the fierce river-demon a bunch of black feathers, a mangy skin with a pendent tail—something that looked like a dried gourd; they shouted periodically together strings of amazing words that resembled no sounds of human language; and the deep murmurs of the crowd, interrupted suddenly, were like the responses of some satanic litany.

"We had carried Kurtz into the pilot-house: there was more air there. Lying on the couch, he stared through the open shutter. There was an eddy in the mass of human bodies, and the woman with helmeted head and tawny cheeks rushed out to the very brink of the stream. She put out her hands, shouted something, and all that wild mob took up the shout in a roaring chorus of articulated, rapid, breathless utterance.

" 'Do you understand this?' I asked.

"He kept on looking out past me with fiery, longing eyes, with a mingled expression of wistfulness and hate. He made no answer, but I saw a smile, a smile of indefinable meaning, appear on his colourless lips that a moment after twitched convulsively. 'Do I not?' he said slowly, gasping, as if the words had been torn out of him by a supernatural power.

"I pulled the string of the whistle, and I did this because I saw the pilgrims on deck getting out their rifles with an air of anticipating a jolly lark. At the sudden screech there was a movement of abject terror through that wedged mass of bodies. 'Don't! don't you frighten them away,' cried someone on deck disconsolately. I pulled the string time after time. They broke and ran, they leaped, they crouched, they swerved, they dodged the flying terror of the sound. The three red chaps had fallen flat, face down on the shore, as though they had been shot dead. Only the barbarous and superb woman did not so much as flinch and stretched tragically her bare arms after us over the sombre and glittering river.

"And then that imbecile crowd down on the deck started their little fun, and I could see nothing more for smoke.

"The brown current ran swiftly out of the heart of darkness, bearing us down towards the sea with twice the speed of our upward progress; and Kurtz's life was running swiftly, too, ebbing, ebbing out of his heart into the sea of inexorable time. The manager was very placid, he had no vital anxieties now, he took us both in with a comprehensive and satisfied glance: the 'affair' had come off as well as could be wished. I saw the time approaching when I would be left alone of the party of 'unsound method.' The pilgrims looked upon me with disfavour. I was, so to speak, numbered with the dead. It is strange how I accepted this unforeseen partnership, this choice of nightmares forced upon me in the tenebrous land invaded by these mean and greedy phantoms.

"Kurtz discoursed. A voice! a voice! It rang deep to the very last. It survived his strength to hide in the magnificent folds of eloquence the barren darkness of his heart. Oh, he struggled! he struggled! The wastes of his weary brain were haunted by shadowy images now—images of wealth and fame revolving obsequiously round his unextinguishable gift of noble and lofty expression. My Intended, my station, my career, my ideas—these were the subjects for the occasional utterances of elevated sentiments. The shade of the original Kurtz frequented the bedside of the hollow sham, whose fate it was to be buried presently in the mould of primeval earth. But both the diabolic love and the unearthly hate of the mysteries it had penetrated fought for the possession of that soul satiated with primitive emotions, avid of lying fame, of sham distinction, of all the appearances of success and power.

"Sometimes he was contemptibly childish. He desired to have kings meet him at railway-stations on his return from some ghastly Nowhere, where he intended to accomplish great things. 'You show them you have in you something that is really profitable, and then there will be no limits to the recognition of your ability,' he would say. 'Of course you must take care of the motives—right motives—always.' The long reaches that were like one and the same reach, monotonous bends that were exactly alike, slipped past the steamer with their multitude of secular trees looking patiently after this grimy fragment of another world, the forerunner of change, of conquest, of trade, of massacres, of blessings. I looked ahead—piloting. 'Close the shutter,' said Kurtz suddenly one day; 'I can't bear to look at this.' I did so. There was a silence. 'Oh, but I will wring your heart yet!' he cried at the invisible wilderness.

"We broke down—as I had expected—and had to lie up for repairs at the head of an island. This delay was the first thing that shook Kurtz's confidence. One morning he gave me a packet of papers and a photograph—the lot tied together with a shoe-string. 'Keep this for me,' he said. 'This noxious fool' (meaning the manager) 'is capable of prying into my boxes when I am not looking.' In the afternoon I saw him. He was lying on his back with closed eyes, and I withdrew quietly, but I heard him mutter, 'Live rightly, die, die . . .' I listened. There was nothing more. Was he rehearsing some speech in his sleep, or was it a fragment of a phrase from some newspaper article? He had been writing for the papers and meant to do so again, 'for the furthering of my ideas. It's a duty.'

"His was an impenetrable darkness. I looked at him as you peer down at a man who is lying at the bottom of a precipice where the sun never shines. But I had not much time to give him, because I was helping the engine-driver to take to pieces the leaky cylinders, to straighten a bent connecting-rod, and in other such matters. I lived in an infernal mess of rust, filings, nuts, bolts, spanners, hammers, ratchet-drills—things I abominate, because I don't get on with them. I tended the little forge we fortunately had aboard; I toiled wearily in a wretched scrap-heap—unless I had the shakes too bad to stand.

"One evening coming in with a candle I was startled to hear him say a little tremulously, 'I am lying here in the dark waiting for death.' The light was within a foot of his eyes. I forced myself to murmur. 'Oh, nonsense!' and stood over him as if transfixed.

"Anything approaching the change that came over his features I have never seen before, and hope never to see again. Oh, I wasn't touched. I was fascinated. It was as though a veil had been rent. I saw on that ivory face the expression of sombre pride, of ruthless power, of craven terror—of an intense and hopeless despair. Did he live his life again in every detail of desire, temptation, and surrender during that supreme moment of complete knowledge? He cried in a whisper at some image, at some vision—he cried out twice, a cry that was no more than a breath—

" 'The horror! The horror!'

"I blew the candle out and left the cabin. The pilgrims were dining in the mess-room, and I took my place opposite the manager, who lifted his eyes to give me a questioning glance, which I successfully ignored. He leaned back, serene, with that peculiar smile of his sealing the unexpressed depths of his meanness. A continuous shower of small flies streamed upon the lamp, upon the cloth, upon our hands and faces. Suddenly the manager's boy put his insolent black head in the doorway, and said in a tone of scathing contempt—

" 'Mistah Kurtz—he dead.'

"All the pilgrims rushed out to see. I remained, and went on with my dinner. I believe I was considered brutally callous. However, I did not eat much. There was a lamp in there—light, don't you know—and outside it was so beastly, beastly dark. I went no more near the remarkable man who had pronounced a judgement upon the adventures of his soul on this earth. The voice was gone. What else had been there? But I am of course aware that next day the pilgrims buried something in a muddy hole.

"And then they very nearly buried me.

"However, as you see, I did not go to join Kurtz there and then. I did not. I remained to dream the nightmare out to the end, and to show my loyalty to Kurtz once more. Destiny. My Destiny! Droll thing life is—that mysterious arrangement of merciless logic for a futile purpose. The most you can hope from it is some knowledge of yourself—that comes too late—a crop of unextinguishable regrets. I have wrestled with death. It is the most unexciting contest you can imagine. It takes place in an impalpable greyness, with nothing underfoot, with nothing around, without spectators, without clamour, without glory, without the great desire of victory, without the great fear of defeat, in a sickly atmosphere of tepid scepticism, without much belief in your own right, and still less in that of your adversary. If such is the form of ultimate wisdom, then life is a greater riddle than some of us think it to be. I was within a hair's-breadth of the last opportunity for pronouncement, and I found with humiliation that probably I would have nothing to say. This is the reason why I affirm that Kurtz was a remarkable man. He had something to say. He said it. Since I had peeped over the edge myself, I understand better the meaning of his stare, that could not see the flame of the candle, but was wide enough to embrace the whole universe, piercing enough to penetrate all the hearts that beat in the darkness. He had summed up—he had judged. 'The horror!' He was a remarkable man. After all, this was the expression of some sort of belief; it had candour, it had conviction, it had a vibrating note of revolt in its whisper, it had the appalling face of a glimpsed truth—the strange commingling of desire and hate. And it is not my own extremity I remember best—a vision of greyness without form filled with physical pain, and a careless contempt for the evanescence of all things—even of this pain itself. No! It is his extremity that I seem to have lived through. True, he had made that last stride, he had stepped over the edge, while I had been permitted to draw back my hesitating foot. And perhaps in this is the whole difference; perhaps all the wisdom, and all truth, and all sincerity, are just compressed into that inappreciable moment of time in which we step over the threshold of the invisible. Perhaps! I like to think my summing-up would not have been a word of careless contempt. Better his cry—much better. It was an affirmation, a moral victory, paid for by innumerable defeats, by abominable terrors, by abominable satisfactions. But it was a victory! That is why I have remained loyal to Kurtz to the last, and even beyond, when a long time after I heard once more, not his own voice, but the echo of his magnificent eloquence thrown to me from a soul as translucently pure as a cliff of crystal.

"No, they did not bury me, though there is a period of time which I remember mistily, with a shuddering wonder, like a passage through some inconceivable world that had no hope in it and no desire. I found myself back in the sepulchral city resenting the sight of people hurrying through the streets to filch a little money from each other, to devour their infamous cookery, to gulp their unwholesome beer, to dream their insignificant and silly dreams. They trespassed upon my thoughts. They were intruders whose knowledge of life was to me an irritating pretence, because I felt so sure they could not possibly know the things I knew. Their bearing, which was simply the bearing of commonplace individuals going about their business in the assurance of perfect safety, was offensive to me like the outrageous flauntings of folly in the face of a danger it is unable to comprehend. I had no particular desire to enlighten them, but I had some difficulty in restraining myself from laughing in their faces, so full of stupid importance. I daresay I was not very well at that time. I tottered about the streets—there were various affairs to settle—grinning bitterly at perfectly respectable persons. I admit my behaviour was inexcusable, but then my temperature was seldom normal in these days. My dear aunt's endeavours to 'nurse up my strength' seemed altogether beside the mark. It was not my strength that wanted nursing, it was my imagination that wanted soothing. I kept the bundle of papers given me by Kurtz, not knowing exactly what to do with it. His mother had died lately, watched over, as I was told, by his Intended. A clean-shaved man, with an official manner and wearing gold-rimmed spectacles, called on me one day and made inquiries, at first circuitous, afterwards suavely pressing, about what he was pleased to denominate certain 'documents.' I was not surprised, because I had had two rows with the manager on the subject out there. I had refused to give up the smallest scrap out of that package, and I took the same attitude with the spectacled man. He became darkly menacing at last, and with much heat argued that the Company had the right to every bit of information about its 'territories.' And said he, 'Mr. Kurtz's knowledge of unexplored regions must have been necessarily extensive and peculiar—owing to his great abilities and to the deplorable circumstances in which he had been placed: therefore—' I assured him Mr. Kurtz's knowledge, however extensive, did not bear upon the problems of commerce or administration. He invoked then the name of science. 'It would be an incalculable loss if,' etc., etc. I offered him the report on the 'Suppression of Savage Customs,' with the postscriptum torn off. He took it up eagerly, but ended by sniffing at it with an air of contempt. 'This is not what we had a right to expect,' he remarked. 'Expect nothing else,' I said. 'There are only private letters.' He withdrew upon some threat of legal proceedings, and I saw him no more; but another fellow, calling himself Kurtz's cousin, appeared two days later, and was anxious to hear all the details about his dear relative's last moments. Incidentally he gave me to understand that Kurtz had been essentially a great musician. 'There was the making of an immense success,' said the man, who was an organist, I believe, with lank grey hair flowing over a greasy coat-collar. I had no reason to doubt his statement; and to this day I am unable to say what was Kurtz's profession, whether he ever had any—which was the greatest of his talents. I had taken him for a painter who wrote for the papers, or else for a journalist who could paint—but even the cousin (who took snuff during the interview) could not tell me what he had been—exactly. He was a universal genius—on that point I agreed with the old chap, who thereupon blew his nose noisily into a large cotton handkerchief and withdrew in senile agitation, bearing off some family letters and memoranda without importance. Ultimately a journalist anxious to know something of the fate of his 'dear colleague' turned up. This visitor informed me Kurtz's proper sphere ought to have been politics 'on the popular side.' He had furry straight eyebrows, bristly hair cropped short, an eye-glass on a broad ribbon, and, becoming expansive, confessed his opinion that Kurtz really couldn't write a bit—'but heavens! how that man could talk. He electrified large meetings. He had faith—don't you see?—he had the faith. He could get himself to believe anything—anything. He would have been a splendid leader of an extreme party.' 'What party?' I asked. 'Any party,' answered the other. 'He was an—an—extremist.' Did I not think so? I assented. Did I know, he asked, with a sudden flash of curiosity, 'what it was that had induced him to go out there?' 'Yes,' said I, and forthwith handed him the famous Report for publication, if he thought fit. He glanced through it hurriedly, mumbling all the time, judged 'it would do,' and took himself off with this plunder.

"Thus I was left at last with a slim packet of letters and the girl's portrait. She struck me as beautiful—I mean she had a beautiful expression. I know that the sunlight can be made to lie, too, yet one felt that no manipulation of light and pose could have conveyed the delicate shade of truthfulness upon those features. She seemed ready to listen without mental reservation, without suspicion, without a thought for herself. I concluded I would go and give her back her portrait and those letters myself. Curiosity? Yes; and also some other feelings perhaps. All that had been Kurtz's had passed out of my hands: his soul, his body, his station, his plans, his ivory, his career. There remained only his memory and his Intended—and I wanted to give that up, too, to the past, in a way—to surrender personally all that remained of him with me to that oblivion which is the last word of our common fate. I don't defend myself. I had no clear perception of what it was I really wanted. Perhaps it was an impulse of unconscious loyalty, or the fulfilment of one of those ironic necessities that lurk in the facts of human existence. I don't know. I can't tell. But I went.

"I thought his memory was like the other memories of the dead that accumulate in every man's life—a vague impress on the brain of shadows that had fallen on it in their swift and final passage; but before the high and ponderous door, between the tall houses of a street as still and decorous as a well-kept alley in a cemetery, I had a vision of him on the stretcher, opening his mouth voraciously, as if to devour all the earth with all its mankind. He lived then before me; he lived as much as he had ever lived—a shadow insatiable of splendid appearances, of frightful realities; a shadow darker than the shadow of the night, and draped nobly in the folds of a gorgeous eloquence. The vision seemed to enter the house with me—the stretcher, the phantom-bearers, the wild crowd of obedient worshippers, the gloom of the forests, the glitter of the reach between the murky bends, the beat of the drum, regular and muffled like the beating of a heart—the heart of a conquering darkness. It was a moment of triumph for the wilderness, an invading and vengeful rush which, it seemed to me, I would have to keep back alone for the salvation of another soul. And the memory of what I had heard him say afar there, with the horned shapes stirring at my back, in the glow of fires, within the patient woods, those broken phrases came back to me, were heard again in their ominous and terrifying simplicity. I remembered his abject pleading, his abject threats, the colossal scale of his vile desires, the meanness, the torment, the tempestuous anguish of his soul. And later on I seemed to see his collected languid manner, when he said one day, 'This lot of ivory now is really mine. The Company did not pay for it. I collected it myself at a very great personal risk. I am afraid they will try to claim it as theirs though. H'm. It is a difficult case. What do you think I ought to do—resist? Eh? I want no more than justice.' . . . He wanted no more than justice—no more than justice, I rang the bell before a mahogany door on the first floor, and while I waited he seemed to stare at me out of the glassy panel—stare with that wide and immense stare embracing, condemning, loathing all the universe. I seemed to hear the whispered cry, 'The horror! The horror!'

"The dusk was falling. I had to wait in a lofty drawing-room with three long windows from floor to ceiling that were like three luminous and bedraped columns. The bent gilt legs and backs of the furniture shone in indistinct curves. The tall marble fireplace had a cold and monumental whiteness. A grand piano stood massively in a corner; with dark gleams on the flat surfaces like a sombre and polished sarcophagus. A high door opened—closed. I rose.

"She came forward, all in black, with a pale head, floating towards me in the dusk. She was in mourning. It was more than a year since his death, more than a year since the news came; she seemed as though she would remember and mourn for ever. She took both my hands in hers and murmured, 'I had heard you were coming.' I noticed she was not very young—I mean not girlish. She had a mature capacity for fidelity, for belief, for suffering. The room seemed to have grown darker, as if all the sad light of the cloudy evening had taken refuge on her forehead. This fair hair, this pale visage, this pure brow, seemed surrounded by an ashy halo from which the dark eyes looked out at me. Their glance was guileless, profound, confident, and trustful. She carried her sorrowful head as though she were proud of that sorrow, as though she would say, I— I alone know how to mourn for him as he deserves. But while we were still shaking hands, such a look of awful desolation came upon her face that I perceived she was one of those creatures that are not the playthings of Time. For her he had died only yesterday. And, by Jove! the impression was so powerful that for me, too, he seemed to have died only yesterday—nay, this very minute, I saw her and him in the same instant of time—his death and her sorrow—I saw her sorrow in the very moment of his death. Do you understand? I saw them together—I heard them together. She had said, with a deep catch of the breath, 'I have survived' while my strained ears seemed to hear distinctly, mingled with her tone of despairing regret, the summing-up whisper of his eternal condemnation. I asked myself what I was doing there, with a sensation of panic in my heart as though I had blundered into a place of cruel and absurd mysteries not fit for a human being to behold. She motioned me to a chair. We sat down. I laid the packet gently on the little table, and she put her hand over it . . . 'You knew him well,' she murmured, after a moment of mourning silence.

" 'Intimacy grows quickly out there,' I said. 'I knew him as well as it is possible for one man to know another.'

" 'And you admired him,' she said. 'It was impossible to know him and not to admire him. Was it?'

" 'He was a remarkable man,' I said, unsteadily. Then before the appealing fixity of her gaze, that seemed to watch for more words on my lips, I went on. 'It was impossible not to—'

" 'Love him,' she finished eagerly, silencing me into an appalled dumbness. 'How true! how true! But when you think that no one knew him so well as I! I had all his noble confidence. I knew him best.'

" 'You knew him best,' I repeated. And perhaps she did. But with every word spoken the room was growing darker, and only her forehead, smooth and white, remained illumined by the unextinguishable light of belief and love.

" 'You were his friend,' she went on. 'His friend,' she repeated, a little louder. 'You must have been, if he had given you this, and sent you to me. I feel I can speak to you—and oh! I must speak. I want you—you who have heard his last words—to know I have been worthy of him . . . It is not pride . . . Yes! I am proud to know I understood him better than anyone on earth—he told me so himself. And since his mother died I have had no one no one—to—to—'

"I listened. The darkness deepened. I was not even sure whether he had given me the right bundle. I rather suspect he wanted me to take care of another batch of his papers which, after his death, I saw the manager examining under the lamp. And the girl talked, easing her pain in the certitude of my sympathy; she talked as thirsty men drink. I had heard that her engagement with Kurtz had been disapproved by her people. He wasn't rich enough or something. And indeed I don't know whether he had not been a pauper all his life. He had given me some reason to infer that it was his impatience of comparative poverty that drove him out there.

" '. . . Who was not his friend who had heard him speak once?' she was saying. 'He drew men towards him by what was best in them.' She looked at me with intensity. 'It is the gift of the great,' she went on, and the sound of her low voice seemed to have the accompaniment of all the other sounds, full of mystery, desolation, and sorrow, I had ever heard—the ripple of the river, the soughing of the trees swayed by the wind, the murmurs of the crowds, the faint ring of incomprehensible words cried from afar, the whisper of a voice speaking from beyond the threshold of an eternal darkness. 'But you have heard him! You know!' she cried.

" 'Yes, I know,' I said with something like despair in my heart, but bowing my head before the faith that was in her, before that great and saving illusion that shone with an unearthly glow in the darkness, in the triumphant darkness from which I could not have defended her—from which I could not even defend myself.

" 'What a loss to me—to us!'—she corrected herself with beautiful generosity; then added in a murmur, 'To the world.' By the last gleams of twilight I could see the glitter of her eyes, full of tears—of tears that would not fall.

" 'I have been very happy—very fortunate—very proud,' she went on. 'Too fortunate. Too happy for a little while. And now I am unhappy for—for life.'

"She stood up; her fair hair seemed to catch all the remaining light in a glimmer of gold. I rose, too.

" 'And of all this,' she went on, mournfully, 'of all his promise, and of all his greatness, of his generous mind, of his noble heart, nothing remains—nothing but a memory. You and I—'

" 'We shall always remember him.' I said, hastily.

" 'No!' she cried. 'It is impossible that all this should be lost—that such a life should be sacrificed to leave nothing—but sorrow. You know what vast plans he had. I knew of them, too—I could not perhaps understand—but others knew of them. Something must remain. His words, at least, have not died.'

" 'His words will remain,' I said.

" 'And his example,' she whispered to herself. 'Men looked up to him—his goodness shone in every act. His example—'

" 'True,' I said; 'his example, too. Yes, his example. I forgot that.'

" 'But I do not. I cannot—I cannot believe—not yet. I cannot believe that I shall never see him again, that nobody will see him again, never, never, never.'

"She put out her arms as if after a retreating figure, stretching them back and with clasped pale hands across the fading and narrow sheen of the window. Never see him! I saw him clearly enough then. I shall see this eloquent phantom as long as I live, and I shall see her, too, a tragic and familiar Shade, resembling in this gesture another one, tragic also, and bedecked with powerless charms, stretching bare brown arms over the glitter of the infernal stream, the stream of darkness She said suddenly very low, 'He died as he lived.'

" 'His end,' said I, with dull anger stirring in me, 'was in every way worthy of his life.'

" 'And I was not with him,' she murmured. My anger subsided before a feeling of infinite pity.

" 'Everything that could be done—' I mumbled.

" 'Ah, but I believed in him more than anyone on earth—more than his own mother, more than—himself. He needed me! Me! I would have treasured every sigh, every word, every sign, every glance.'

"I felt like a chill grip on my chest. 'Don't,' I said, in a muffled voice.

" 'Forgive me. I—I—have mourned so long in silence—in silence . . . You were with him—to the last? I think of his loneliness. Nobody near to understand him as I would have understood. Perhaps no one to hear . . .'

" 'To the very end,' I said, shakily. 'I heard his very last words . . .' I stopped in a fright.

" 'Repeat them,' she murmured in a heart-broken tone. 'I want—I want—something—something—to—to live with.'

"I was on the point of crying at her, 'Don't you hear them?' The dusk was repeating them in a persistent whisper all around us, in a whisper that seemed to swell menacingly like the first whisper of a rising wind. 'The horror! The horror!'

" 'His last word—to live with,' she insisted. 'Don't you understand I loved him—I loved him—I loved him!'

"I pulled myself together and spoke slowly.

" 'The last word he pronounced was—your name.'

"I heard a light sigh and then my heart stood still, stopped dead short by an exulting and terrible cry, by the cry of inconceivable triumph and of unspeakable pain. 'I knew it—I was sure!' . . . She knew. She was sure. I heard her weeping; she had hidden her face in her hands. It seemed to me that the house would collapse before I could escape, that the heavens would fall upon my head. But nothing happened. The heavens do not fall for such a trifle. Would they have fallen, I wonder, if I had rendered Kurtz that justice which was his due? Hadn't he said he wanted only justice? But I couldn't. I could not tell her. It would have been too dark—too dark altogether . . ."

Marlow ceased, and sat apart, indistinct and silent, in the pose of a meditating Buddha. Nobody moved for a time. "We have lost the first of the ebb,' said the Director, suddenly. I raised my head. The offing was barred by a black bank of clouds, and the tranquil waterway leading to the uttermost ends of the earth flowed sombre under an overcast sky—seemed to lead into the heart of an immense darkness.

SELECTIONS FROM THE CONGO DIARY

"On the road to-day passed a skeleton tied up to a post. Also white man's grave—No name."

Conrad was to take command of a steamer in Kinshasa in August 1890. He kept a diary during this period—the first notes, in effect, for Heart of Darkness, *which was composed at the end of that decade. The following pages excerpt Conrad's account of his arduous 230-mile journey overland in the Belgian Congo from Matadi to Nselemba, where he stopped a beating and examined a youth with a gunshot wound to the head.*

ABBREVIATIONS

acquain^{ce}: acquaintance
after^{ds}: afterwards
av^{ge}: average
camp^{g}: camping
camp^{g}: camping
com^{al}: commercial
compy: company
dist^{ce}: distance
E^{d}: eastward
est^{d}: estimated
gov^{t}: government
gov^{t}: government
H.: Harou
missio.: missionaries
mket: market
Nth: north
offer: officer
sta^{on}: station
Sth: south
v.g.: very good

Arrived at Matadi on the 13th of June 1890.—

Mr Gosse chief of the station (O.K.) retaining us for some reason of his own.

Made the acquaintance of Mr Roger Casement, which I should consider as a great pleasure under any circumstances and now it becomes a positive piece of luck.

Thinks, speaks well, most intelligent and very sympathetic.—

Feel considerably in doubt about the future. Think just now that my life amongst the people (white) around here can not be very comfortable. Intend avoid acquaintances as much as possible.

Through Mr R.C. Have made the acquain^{ce} of Mr Underwood the manager of the English factory (Hatton & Cookson, in Kalla Kalla. Av^{ge} com^{al}—Hearty and kind. Lunched there on the 21st.—

24th Gosse and R.C. gone with a large lot of ivory down to Boma. On G. return intend to start up the river. Have been myself busy packing ivory in casks. Idiotic employment. Health good up to now.

Wrote to Simpson, to Gov.B. to Purd. to Hope, to Cap Froud, and to Mar. Prominent characteristic of the social life here: People speaking ill of each other.—

. . .

Saturday 28th June left Matadi with Mr Harou and a caravan of 31 men. Parted with Casement in a very friendly manner. Mr Gosse saw us off as far as the State station.—
    First halt. M'poso. 2 Danes in Compny.

Sund. 29th. Ascent of Palaballa. Sufficiently fatiguing—Camped at 11ʰ am at Nsoke-River. Mosquitos.

Monday. 30th to Congo da Lemba after passing black rocks long ascent. Harou giving up. Bother. Camp bad. Water far. Dirty. At night Harou better.

1st July.
    Tuesday. 1st. Left early in a heavy mist marching towards Lufu River.—Part route through forest on the sharp slope of a high mountain. Very long descent. Then, market place, from where short walk to the bridge (good) and camp. V.G. Bath. Clear river. Feel well Harou all right. 1st chicken. 2p.[m]
    No sunshine to day—

Wednesday 2ᵈ July—
    Started at 5ʰ 30 after a sleepless night. Country more open— Gently andulating hills. Road good in perfect order. (District of Lukungu). Great market at 9.30. bought eggs & chickens—
    Feel not well to day. Heavy cold in the head. Arrived at 11ʰ at Banza Manteka. Camped on the market place. Not well enough to call on the missionary. Water scarce and bad—Campᵍ place dirty.—
    2 Danes still in company

Thursday 3ᵈ July.
    Left at 6am. after a good night's rest. Crossed a low range of hills and entered a broad valley or rather plain with a break in the middle—Met an offer of the State inspecting. A few minutes afterwards saw at a campᵍ place the dead body of a Backongo. Shot? Hor-

rid smell.—Crossed a range of mountains running NW-SE. by a low pass. Another broad flat valley with a deep ravine through the centre.—Clay and gravel. Another range parallel to the first-mentioned with a chain of low foothills running close to it. Between the two came to camp on the banks of Luinzono River. Camp^g place clean. River clear. Gov^t. Zanzibari with register. Canoe. 2 danes camp^g on the other bank.—Health good.

General tone of landscape grey yellowish (Dry grass) with reddish patches (Soil) and clumps of dark green vegetation scattered sparsely about. Mostly in steep gorges between the higher mountains or in ravines cutting the plain—Noticed Palma Christi—Oil palm. Very straight tall and thick trees in some places. Name not known to me. Villages quite invisible. Infer their existence from calbashes suspended to palm trees for the 'malafu'.

Good many caravans and travellers. No women unless on the market place.—

Bird notes charming—One especially a flute-like note. Another kind of 'boom' resembling the very distant baying of a hound.— Saw only pigeons and a few green parroquets; very small and not many No birds of prey seen by me. Up to 9am—sky clouded and calm—Afterwards gentle breeze from the Nth generally and sky clearing—Nights damp and cool.—White mists on the hills up about halfway. Water effects, very beautiful this morning. Mists generally raising before sky clears.

Friday—4th July.—

Left camp at 6^h am—after a very unpleasant night—Marching across a chain of hills and then in a maze of hills—At 8.15 opened out into an andulating plain Took bearings of a break in the chain of mountains on the other side—Bearing NNE—Road passes through that Sharp ascents up very steep hills not very high. The higher mountains recede sharply and show a low hilly country—

At 9.30 Market place.

At 10^h passed R. Lukanga and at 10.30 Camped on the Mpwe R.

Saw another dead body lying by the path in an attitude of med
itative repose.—

In the evening 3 women of whom one albino passed our camp—
Horrid chalky white with pink blotches. Red eyes. Red hair. Features very negroid and ugly.—

Mosquitos. At night when the moon rose heard shouts and
drumming in distant villages Passed a bad night.

Saturday 5th July. 90.

Left at 6.15. Morning cool, even cold and very damp—Sky
densely overcast. Gentle breeze from NE. Road through a narrow
plain up to R. Kwilu. Swift flowing and deep 50 yds wide—Passed in
canoes—After^{ds} up and down very steep hills intersected by deep
ravines—Main chain of heights running mostly NW-SE or W
and E at times. Stopped at Manyamba—Camp^g place bad—in a
hollow—Water very indifferent. Tent set at 10^h 15^m

To day fell into a muddy puddle. Beastly. The fault of the man
that carried me. After camp^g went to a small stream bathed and
washed clothes.—Getting jolly well sick of this fun.—

Tomorrow expect a long march to get to Nsona. 2 days from
Manyanga.—

No sunshine to-day.

Sunday 6th July—

Started at 5.40.—the route at first hilly then after a sharp descent
traversing a broad plain. At the end of it a large market place.

At 10^h sun came out.—

After leaving the market passed another plain then walking on
the crest of a chain of hills passed 2 villages and at 11^h arrived at
Nsona.—Village invisible—

In this camp (Nsona—) there is a good camp^{g}place. Shady. Water
far and not very good.—This night no mosquitos owing to large
fires lit all round our tent.—

Afternoon very close
Night clear and starry.

. . .

Monday-7ᵗʰ July.—

Left at 6ʰ after a good night's rest on the road to Inkandu which is some distance past Lukungu govᵗ station.—

Route very accidented. Succession of round steep hills. At times walking along the crest of a chain of hills.—

Just before Lukunga our carriers took a wide sweep to the southward till the station bore Nᵗʰ.—Walking through long grass for 1½ hours.—Crossed a broad river about 100 feet wide and 4 deep.—After another ½ hours walk through manioc plantations in good order rejoined our route to the Eᵈ of the Lukunga Staᵒⁿ Walking along an undulating plain towards the Inkandu market on a hill.—Hot, thirsty and tired. At 11ʰ arrived on the marketplace—About 200 people.—Business brisk. No water. No campᵍ place—After remaining for one hour left in search of a resting place.—

Row with carriers.—No water. At last about 1½ p.m. camped on an exposed hill side near a muddy creek. No shade. Tent on a slope. Sun heavy. Wretched.

Night miserably cold.

No sleep. Mosquitos—

Tuesday 8th July

Left at 6ʰ am

About ten minutes from camp left main govᵗ path for the Manyanga track. Sky overcast. Road up and down all the time—Passing a couple of villages

The country presents a confused wilderness of hills land slips on their sides showing red. Fine effect of red hill covered in places by dark green vegetation

½ hour before beginning the descent got a glimpse of the Congo.—Sky clouded.

Arrived at Manyanga at 9ʰa.m.

Received most kindly by Mssrs Heyn & Jaeger.—

Most comfortable and pleasant halt.—

Stayed here till the 25. Both have been sick.—Most kindly care taken of us. Leave with sincere regret.

(Mafiela)

Frid^y 25th	—	Nkenghe	—	left
Sat. 26		Nsona		Nkendo K
Sund. 27		Nkandu		Luasi
Mond 28		Nkonzo		Nzungi (Ngoma)
Tues. 29		Nkenghe		Inkissi
Wedn: 30		Nsona	mercredi —	Stream
Thurs: 31.		Nkandu		Luila
Frid^y 1st Aug.		Nkonzo		Nselemba
Sat^y 2^d		Nkenghe		
Sund. 3^d		Nsona		
Mond. 4th		Nkandu		
Tues^d: 5th		Nkonzo.		
Wedn^y 6th		Nkenghe.		

Friday the 25th July 1890.—

Left Manyanga at 2½ p.m—with plenty of hammock carriers. H. lame and not in very good form. Myself ditto but not lame. Walked as far as Mafiela and camped—2^h

Saturday—26th

Left very early—Road ascending all the time.—Passed villages. Country seems thickly inhabited. At 11^h arrived at large Market place. Left at noon and camped at 1^h pm.

Sunday. 27th

Left at 8^h am. Sent luggage carriers straight on to Luasi and went ourselves round by the Mission of Sutili.

Hospitable reception by Mrs Comber—all the missio. absent.—

The looks of the whole establishment eminently civilized and very refreshing to see after the lots of tumble down hovels in which the state & company agents are content to live.—

Fine buildings. Position on a hill. Rather breezy.—

Left at 3^h pm. At the first heavy ascent met Mr Davis Miss. returning from a preaching trip. Rev. Bentley away in the south with his wife.—

This being off the road no section given—Distance traversed about 15 miles—Gen. Direction ENE.—

At Luasi we get on again on to the gov.^t road.—

Camped at 4½ pm. with Mr Heche in company.—

To day no sunshine—

Wind remarkably cold—

Gloomy day.—

Monday. 28th

Left camp at 6.30 after breakfasting with Heche—

Road at first hilly. Then walking along the ridges of hill chains with valleys on both sides.—The country more open and there is much more trees growing in large clumps in the ravines.—

Passed Nzungi and camped 11^h on the right bank of Ngoma. A rapid little river with rocky bed. Village on a hill to the right.—

No sunshine. Gloomy cold day. Squalls.

Tuesday—29th

Left camp at 7^h after a good night's rest. Continuous ascent; rather easy at first.—Crossed wooded ravines and the river Lunzadi by a very decent bridge—

At 9^h met Mr Louette escorting a sick agent of the Comp^y back to Matadi—Looking very well—Bad news from up the river—All the steamers disabled. One wrecked.—Country wooded—At 10.30 camped at Inkissi

Sun visible at 6.30. Very warm day.—

29th

Inkissi River very rapid, is about 100 yards broad—Passage in canoes.—Banks wooded very densely and valley of the river rather deep but very narrow.—

To day did not set the tent but put up in gov^t shimbek. Zanzibari in charge—Very obliging.—Met ripe pineapple for the first time.—

On the road to day passed a skeleton tied-up to a post. Also white man's grave—No name. heap of stones in the form of a cross.

Health good now—

. . .

Wednesday—30th.

Left at 6 am intending to camp at Kinfumu—Two hours sharp walk brought me to Nsona na Nsefe—Market—½ hour after Harou arrived very ill with billious attack and fever.—Laid him down in gov.ᵗ shimbek—Dose of Ipeca. Vomiting bile in enormous quantities. At 11ʰ gave him 1 gramme of quinine and lots of hot tea. Hot fit ending in heavy perspiration. At 9ʰ p.m. put him in hammock and started for Kinfumu—Row with carriers all the way. Harou suffering much through the jerks of the hammock Camped at a small stream.—

At 4ʰ Harou better. Fever gone.—

Up till noon, sky clouded and strong NW wind very chilling. From 1ʰ pm to 4ʰ pm sky clear and very hot day. Expect lots of battles with carriers to-morrow—Had them all called and made a speech which they did not understand. They promise good behaviour

Thursday—31st

Left at 6ʰ—Sent Harou ahead and followed in ½ an hour.—Road presents several sharp ascents and a few others easier but rather long. Notice in places sandy surface soil instead of hard clay as heretofore; think however that the layer of sand is not very thick and that the clay would be found under it. Great difficulty in carrying Harou.—Too heavy. Bother! Made two long halts to rest the carriers. Country wooded in valleys and on many of the ridges.

At 2.30 pm reached Luila at last and camped on right bank.— Breeze from SW

General direction of march about NE½E

Distance estᵈ —16 miles

Congo very narrow and rapid. Kinzilu rushing in. A short distance up from the mouth fine waterfall.—

—Sun rose red—From 9ʰa.m. infernally hot day.—

Harou very little better.

Self rather seedy. Bathed.

Luila about 60 feet wide. Shallow

. . .

<u>Friday—1st of August 1890</u>

Left at 6.30 am after a very indifferently passed night—Cold, Heavy mists—Road in long ascents and sharp dips all the way to Mfumu Mbé—

After leaving there a long and painful climb up a very steep hill; then a long descent to Mfumu Koko where a long halt was made.

Left at 12.30pm—towards Nselemba. Many ascents—The aspect of the country entirely changed—Wooded hills with openings.— Path almost all the afternoon thro a forest of light trees with dense undergrowth.—

After a halt on a wooded hillside reached Nselemba at 4^h 10^m pm.

Put up at gov^t shanty.—

Row between the carriers and a man stating himself in gov^t employ, about a mat.—Blows with sticks raining hard—Stopped it. Chief came with a youth about 13 suffering from gunshot wound in the head. Bullet entered about an inch above the right eyebrow and came out a little inside the roots of the hair, fairly in the middle of the brow in a line with the bridge of the nose—Bone not damaged apparently. Gave him a little glycerine to put on the wound made by the bullet on coming out.

Harou not very well. Mosquitos—Frogs—Beastly. Glad to see the end of this stupid tramp. Feel rather seedy.

Sun rose red—Very hot day—Wind S<u>th</u>.

<u>General direction of march — EbyN</u>

<u>Distance about   17 miles</u>

Grateful acknowledgment is made to the following for permission to reprint previously published material:

CHINUA ACHEBE: Excerpts from "An Image of Africa: Racism in Conrad's *Heart of Darkness*" by Chinua Achebe (*The Massachusetts Review*, Vol. XVIII, No. 4, Winter 1977). Reprinted by permission of Chinua Achebe.

THE BERTRAND RUSSELL PEACE FOUNDATION LTD.: Excerpt from "Joseph Conrad" from *Portraits from Memory and Other Essays* by Bertrand Russell. Reprinted by permission of The Bertrand Russell Peace Foundation Ltd.

DOUBLEDAY, A DIVISION OF RANDOM HOUSE, INC., AND WALKER MARTINEAU AS TRUSTEES OF THE JOSEPH CONRAD ESTATE: Excerpts from "The Congo Diary" from *Last Essays* by Joseph Conrad. Copyright © 1926 by Doubleday, a division of Random House, Inc. Rights outside of the United States are controlled by Walker Martineau as Trustees of the Joseph Conrad Estate. Reprinted by permission of Doubleday, a division of Random House, Inc., and Walker Martineau as Trustees of the Joseph Conrad Estate.

FARRAR, STRAUS & GIROUX, INC.: Excerpt from *We Wish to Inform You that Tomorrow We Will Be Killed with Our Families: Stories from Rwanda* by Philip Gourevitch. Copyright © 1998 by Philip Gourevitch. Reprinted by permission of Farrar, Straus & Giroux, Inc.

HARCOURT, INC.: Excerpt from "Joseph Conrad: A Note" from *Abinger Harvest* by Edward M. Forster. Copyright © 1936 and renewed 1964 by Edward M. Forster. Excerpt from "Mr. Conrad: A Conversation" from *The Captain's Death and Other Essays* by Virginia Woolf. Copyright © 1950 and renewed 1978 by Harcourt, Inc. All excerpts reprinted by permission of the publisher.

HARVARD UNIVERSITY PRESS: Excerpts from *Sincerity and Authenticity* by Lionel Trilling (Cambridge, MA: Harvard University Press, 1972). Copyright © 1971, 1972 by the President and Fellows of Harvard College. Reprinted by permission of the publisher.

SIMON AND SCHUSTER, INC.: Excerpt "Conrad, Optimist and Moralist" from *By-Line: Ernest Hemingway* edited by William White. Copyright © 1967 by Mary Hemingway. Originally appeared in *Transatlantic Review*. Reprinted by permission of Simon and Schuster, Inc.

A Note on the Type

The principal text of this Modern Library edition
was set in a digitized version of Janson,
a typeface that dates from about 1690 and was cut by Nicholas Kis,
a Hungarian working in Amsterdam. The original matrices have
survived and are held by the Stempel foundry in Germany.
Hermann Zapf redesigned some of the weights and sizes for Stempel,
basing his revisions on the original design.

MODERN LIBRARY IS ONLINE AT
WWW.MODERNLIBRARY.COM

MODERN LIBRARY ONLINE IS YOUR GUIDE TO CLASSIC LITERATURE ON THE WEB

THE MODERN LIBRARY E-NEWSLETTER

Our free e-mail newsletter is sent to subscribers, and features sample chapters, interviews with and essays by our authors, upcoming books, special promotions, announcements, and news.

To subscribe to the Modern Library e-newsletter, send a blank e-mail to: sub_modernlibrary@info.randomhouse.com or visit www.modernlibrary.com

THE MODERN LIBRARY WEBSITE

Check out the Modern Library website at
www.modernlibrary.com for:

- The Modern Library e-newsletter
- A list of our current and upcoming titles and series
- Reading Group Guides and exclusive author spotlights
- Special features with information on the classics and other paperback series
- Excerpts from new releases and other titles
- A list of our e-books and information on where to buy them
- The Modern Library Editorial Board's 100 Best Novels and 100 Best Nonfiction Books of the Twentieth Century written in the English language
- News and announcements

Questions? E-mail us at modernlibrary@randomhouse.com.
For questions about examination or desk copies, please visit
the Random House Academic Resources site at
www.randomhouse.com/academic

Author tells a story
through character
eventually we are
spoken to. appealing
direct.

OSAMA BIN LADEN

The Company.